WORTH THE WAIT

OAK BROOK ACADEMY, BOOK 4

JILLIAN ADAMS

JILLIANADAMS.COM

ONE

"Get a room." I rolled my eyes as I shoved past Mick and Alana. "You're blocking the table!"

"Sorry, Maby." Mick grinned as he pulled away from Alana.

Alana hopped off the edge of the table and settled on the bench instead. "Mick's been so busy with football we've hardly had any time together."

"Sure, sure." I sat down at the table and did my best to hold back my opinion. Maybe a little time apart would do them some good. They'd both gotten so wrapped up in each other lately that I couldn't tell where one ended and the other began. "Just behave yourselves—I don't want you being a bad influence on Oliver."

"Oliver? That's his name?" Candy sat down beside me, her hair pulled back in pigtails that bounced cheerfully above each of her shoulders. "I can't wait to meet him. Do you think he'll be nice? I hear people from England can be a little snotty."

"Snotty?" Wes sat down on the other side of me. "I'm not sure if that's the case or if they just don't like Americans."

"This is what I'm talking about!" I slapped my hands together. "You can't behave this way when Oliver arrives. We need to make him feel welcome. He's a transfer and he's going to need a lot of help adjusting once he gets here. Besides, everyone knows that people from England are far more cultured and polite than any American."

"I'm not sure I agree with that." Chuckles frowned as he looked across the table at me.

"You don't have to agree with it." I shrugged. "Just don't give Oliver a hard time. I'm sure he's going to be shy and over-whelmed with the culture shock of being here. We should all do our best to help him fit in and give him the support he's going to need."

"Maby is right." Apple stretched her arms above her head, revealing a stripe of orange paint on the inside of her wrist. "The least we can do is offer him a warm welcome."

"Have you and Ty been playing around in the art closet again?" I sighed as I stared at the splotches of paint scattered across her uniform shirt.

"Uh, no." Her cheeks reddened as she looked down at her tray.

"Sure." I rolled my eyes and grinned.

As happy as I was for my friends that had broken off into couples lately, I also found it a little irritating. The puppy love that surrounded me was hard to ignore. Mick already had his arm around Alana again and Wes had pulled Fifi into his lap the moment she arrived at the table.

It was hard for me not to notice that I was the odd one out compared to the majority of my friends. But I wasn't jealous. Instead, I felt lucky. At least I'd managed to avoid the pitfalls of high school love. Next year I'd graduate and then my life could begin when I went off to college. There I had a better chance of making a real, lasting connection—but, of course, not until at least my junior year.

"When is Oliver supposed to arrive?" Wes fed Fifi a French fry from his plate.

"Sometime today. It was supposed to be this morning, but I guess there was some kind of delay." I glanced at my phone. "I'll get a text when he arrives."

"It's so nice of you to do this." Candy popped open her bottle of water and took a long sip.

"I'm looking forward to it." I smiled. "I'm sure he'll have plenty to tell me about England. I've been there a few times myself, but it's always good to get the view of a real local."

"Oh please, I know it's the accent you're looking forward to." Mick grinned. "Ladies love those accents."

"Grow up." I sighed as I stood up from the table. "I'm not swayed by an accent."

"No?" Wes glanced up at her. "Even if he offers to share his chips?" He attempted an English accent.

"What is that supposed to be?" I laughed. "You sound like you have something stuck in your throat."

"Ouch, harsh." Wes winked at me, then grinned at Fifi. "It was pretty good right?"

"Sorry, I'm going to have to go with Maby on this one." She scrunched up her nose. "I was about to ask if you were choking."

"Ha, ha." He shot Fifi a playful glare.

"Oops, looks like I just got that text." I pretended to check a text on my phone as Wes pulled Fifi into a passionate kiss.

As I hurried toward the door of the cafeteria, I ignored a subtle burst of jealousy in my chest. No, I wasn't the least bit interested in Wes, but would it really be so terrible to have someone to share everything with? It seemed that since most of my friends had partnered up, I had a lot of free time, which allowed my mind to wander a little too much.

Helping Oliver adjust to life at Oak Brook Academy—home

for me and my friends in New York City—would be a great distraction. If only he would actually arrive.

I checked my phone again. With only a few hours of school left, I began to wonder if he would even show up.

Ever since I'd received the news of his transfer, I'd imagined what he might be like. I was sure that he'd be sophisticated, at least far more sophisticated than any of the boys at Oak Brook. Although I hated to admit that Mick was right, I also looked forward to his accent. Mostly, I was curious about having a new friend.

I'd made so many friends while attending boarding school. We were a makeshift family, but there was always room for more. I tried to picture myself in his place, coming to a new country, with no friends or family nearby. Would I be scared? I smiled to myself as I walked in the direction of the main office.

"Not a chance." I shook my head. I'd be thrilled to be in a new place.

Just as I reached the door to the main office, my phone buzzed with a text. "Ah, Oliver has arrived." I smiled as I pulled open the door. My mind buzzed with excitement at the idea of meeting him. Something new, something different in my life. Things had become way too routine lately. I needed something to shake my life up.

I stepped into the office and found the receptionist behind her desk.

"Maby, that was fast." She smiled at me. "Eager to meet Oliver, are you?"

"You could say that." I laughed, then glanced around the office. "Where is he?"

"Well, he was right here, but as soon as he finished his paperwork he took off. I told him to wait for you, but he didn't listen." She pointed to the door. "He can't be far if you want to try to catch up with him."

"Didn't you tell him that I would show him around?" I frowned.

"I did." She winced, then lowered her voice. "He didn't seem terribly interested in the idea."

"Oh." I narrowed my eyes. "Alright, I'll track him down."

"Good luck, I think you're going to need it." She shook her head, then turned back to her computer.

I stepped back out of the office, my hopes for excitement slightly dashed. Why wouldn't he wait for me? As I rounded the corner to the next hallway, my phone buzzed. I looked down at it in the same moment that I bumped into another person in the hallway.

"Pardon me."

That accent.

I looked up and into light brown eyes that seemed to be flecked with hints of green. "Sorry, I wasn't looking."

"This might be the problem." He pointed at the phone in my hand. "Don't you Yanks know not to text and walk at the same time?"

My eyes widened as I tucked my phone into my pocket. "Don't you Brits know it's not polite to stand a person up?"

TWO

Oliver folded his arms across his chest and stared at me with a faint smile.

"Cheeky, aren't you?"

"Cheeky?" I narrowed my eyes. "More like rightfully annoyed."

"I thought you'd be relieved. I'm sure a girl like you has a lot more to do with her time than spend it on some strange bloke." He ran his hand back over his short black hair. "I didn't mean to get you ruffled."

"I think we got off to the wrong start." I thrust my hand out toward him. "I'm Maby. I mean, Mabel."

"Well, which is it?" He took my hand in a brief shake.

"My friends call me Maby." I let my hand fall back to my side. "And you're Oliver, right?"

"All over." He ran his hand across his chest, then laughed.

I did my best not to cringe. "Nice to meet you."

"Sorry, it's a cheesy joke, I know." His cheeks reddened some. "Usually it gets a laugh, though."

"It's cute." I forced a smile, then took a breath. "Okay, well, now that we've officially been introduced, I can't wait to show you around Oak Brook Academy. There really is so much to do here and the people are pretty great." I wrapped my arm around his and began to lead him down the hall. "Since you arrived so late, we'll have to squeeze it all in before the end of the day, but don't worry, I can do that."

"Okay." His arm tensed, but he didn't pull it away.

"Here we have the cafeteria. I know it's usually the worst part of a school, but at Oak Brook, it's pretty great. The chef will take custom orders—including vegan and gluten-free—and there are food options from around the world." I waved to one of the cafeteria staff members. "You just missed lunch, but if you're hungry, I'm sure the chef will whip something up for you."

"No thanks." He shrugged. "At my school back home, we were encouraged to cook our own food harvested from our garden. Do you have a garden here?"

"Well, there is a horticulture club and they do have a garden, but I don't think anyone gets their lunch from it."

"Shame. What's the point of having a garden then? I prefer fresh food. I suppose it will have to do for now." He frowned.

"Trust me, the food is very fresh."

"Not as fresh as picking it from the garden, hm?"

"I'll tell you what, I can hook you up with the president of the horticulture club and I'm sure he'll give you permission to take whatever you'd like from the garden."

"I wouldn't touch it." He scrunched up his nose. "Not unless it's organic."

"I'm sure it is."

"No—I mean actually organic. Everyone says their garden is organic, but most people have no idea what that actually means." He rolled his eyes.

"I'm sure you could discuss that with Kyle. He's in charge of the club." I bit into my bottom lip. Although it was nice to listen to Oliver's accent, I wasn't so sure about his attitude. Then again, I'd been told that I could be a little difficult myself. "What other kinds of interests do you have? I'm sure we can find something here that you'd enjoy."

"I doubt that." He stood at the edge of the football field and shook his head. "There's nothing here that interests me—or that will probably ever interest me." He glanced at me. "It's a nice enough school, don't get me wrong, but it can't compare to what I'm used to."

"I can understand that, I guess. But you haven't even given it a chance. Tell me one thing you're interested in and I'll bet we can at least come close to finding it here."

"Alright, fine." He drew a deep breath, then sighed. "I guess what I'll miss the most is my rides. The stables at my old school are full of thoroughbred horses that are well-trained and fast."

"Ah, now that's something I can help you with." I grinned as I tightened my grasp on his arm.

"Seriously? This place doesn't seem big enough to have horses."

"They're not on the property, but Oak Brook does have a deal with a nearby stable. Students are allowed to ride the horses as often as they want as long as they've taken lessons. But in your case, I'm sure you can prove that you're an expert rider without having to go through the classes. I'll get permission for us to spend part of the day tomorrow over there. It's a bit of a ride, but worth it." I patted his arm. "See? A reason to smile—finally."

"We'll see." He frowned. "I won't take any chances on a lame horse."

I tightened my lips. I'd been trying to tolerate his attitude, but my patience had begun to grow thin. As I led him in the direction of the stables, my frustration brewed. I decided to try to make an effort to make him feel welcome, even if his attitude was a bit off-putting.

"I bet it's been rough leaving everything behind back home." I flashed a smile at him. "I've been attending school here since my freshman year, so I'm used to living away from home."

"I've been in boarding schools since kindergarten." He glanced over at me. "I prefer it. Besides, my parents are always off traveling; I'd be home alone most of the time if I wasn't away at school."

"What about any siblings?" I led him through the entrance of the dormitories. "Or are you an only child?"

"I have an older brother, but he's much older; we didn't really grow up together." He shrugged. "I guess you could say that I'm an only child in a sense."

"So am I." I nodded. "My mother likes to say that she didn't want to mess with perfection."

"Really? I've heard that most parents of only children stop at one because their child is very difficult."

"Wow, seriously?" I turned to look at him.

"Have you ever asked?" He raised an eyebrow as his lips twitched upward into a smile.

"Do people in England find your attitude endearing?" I shook my head.

"Some, yes." He shifted closer to me, his eyes locked to mine. "Why?"

"I'm starting to think there's a reason you were shipped off." I rolled my eyes.

"Harsh." He turned to look at me, his lips pushed into a faint pout. "I thought you were my welcoming party?"

"Welcome." I gestured to the room around us. "This is the common room—a good place to make new friends. Enjoy!" I gave him a short wave, then headed off down the hall to the girls' dormitory. Already, I'd had enough of his attitude. I did try to have patience, but when it came to certain types of behavior, I just couldn't manage it most of the time. When I opened the door to my dorm room, I found my roommate Fifi at the kitchen table with a bowl of cereal.

"What are you eating?" I laughed as I watched her scoop up a large bite.

"Don't judge, I'm starving." She grinned.

"No judgment from me, as long as you don't call me cheeky." I sat down across from her and sighed.

"Sounds like things with Oliver didn't go too well?"

"He's just not what I expected. I guess in my mind I imagined a dapper gentleman and what I got is a sullen and sarcastic teenage boy. I could get that anywhere I look at Oak Brook!"

"But he does have an accent, right?" Fifi laughed. "So that should make up for it."

"Accents aren't everything." I tipped my head back and forth. "But yes; yes, he does have an accent." I decided not to mention just how delicious it was.

"I can't wait to meet him."

"Trust me, you can and you should." I rolled my eyes.

"Hm, we'll see. Maybe he's just nervous. This place is brand new to him. I know it was pretty overwhelming to me when I first arrived here. Give him some time." She took another bite of her cereal.

"Maybe." I frowned. "I'll do my best."

"I know you will."

THREE

When I woke up the next morning, Fifi's words lingered in my mind. Maybe she was right that I'd been too quick to judge Oliver. After all, he had just arrived not only to a new school but to a new country entirely. Maybe I needed to give him more time to adjust. I could start with proving to him that we had access to some of the most beautiful and skilled horses in the entire state of New York.

After placing a call to the principal to get permission, I headed off through the courtyard to hunt down Oliver. Most of the kids at Oak Brook would spend their weekends in the city, but in order to leave the campus they had to get permission and travel in pairs or groups. Armed with permission to head out for the day, I just had to find my companion.

As I neared a gathering of girls, I heard a familiar accent from the middle of the group.

"Sure, there are nice things about the U.S., but England has everything that you could ever want. Plus me." He laughed. The girls around him laughed too.

I tried not to puke.

"The U.S. has you right now." I shouldered my way through

the group of girls and smirked. "Me in particular. You and I have permission to go out for the day."

"Oh? I didn't realize that dating was arranged here." He narrowed his eyes. "Are you sure you're in the right country?"

"It's not a date." I frowned as I heard a few of the girls whisper around me. "It's an opportunity. I'd like to show you just how enjoyable it can be to be here." I crossed my arms. "Unless you'd rather stay here and show off your accent, that is."

"Stay!" one of the girls beside me squeaked, then giggled.

I noticed a flicker of annoyance cross Oliver's face. How could he be annoyed if their attention was what he wanted?

"Sure. I'm curious enough to find out what you have in mind. I'll see you later, ladies." He winked at them, then fell into step beside me. "So where are we headed?"

"To the stables." I flashed our pass at the guard near the entrance of the school. "We have as long as we want."

"Thrilling." He shoved his hands in his pockets. "I thought you would plan something more adventurous."

"I'm just trying to make you feel a little more comfortable here."

"I'm never going to be comfortable here."

"You seemed pretty comfortable back there." I glanced over at him as I hailed a taxi.

"Did I?" He looked straight into my eyes.

The sudden direct eye contact startled me, as did the anguish that I noticed.

"Oliver, are you okay?"

He pulled open the door of the taxi for me. "Ladies first."

I stared at him as I settled inside the taxi. Once I gave the directions to the driver, I turned to look at him. His smirk was back as he sprawled across the seat, his arm loosely draped above my shoulders. Had I imagined what I'd seen?

"So, this is the big city." He gazed out the window at the buildings we passed. "Not so impressive."

"It has its perks."

"Does it?" He glanced over at me. "What are your favorite spots?"

"I have a few. But one in particular is a really interesting place to visit. Maybe I'll take you sometime." I looked down at my hands folded in my lap. Thinking of that spot made me think of Jennifer. It had been so long since I'd heard from my old roommate. I wondered if she'd ever contact me again.

"Are you going to tell me where it is?"

"Maybe." I looked over at him. "Are you going to drop this tough guy act and be who you really are?"

"You think I'm tough?" He smiled. "I like that about you."

"Nice." I looked out the window and sighed.

It wasn't too long before the buildings disappeared and were replaced by a more country setting. Then the taxi turned down a long road that led to the stables.

"Shady Meadows?" He read the large sign as we passed it. "How quaint."

"Trust me, it's a great place." I paid the driver, then stepped out of the taxi.

"Maybe you should wait. I may not want to be here long." Oliver met the driver's eyes.

"You want me to wait or go?" He frowned. "I get paid either way."

"Go." I shot a look at Oliver. "You'll survive."

"So you say." He groaned as the cab drove away and we made our way toward the stables.

I smiled at the young man who was walking toward me. Well, I couldn't help but smile. Aaron, the horseback riding instructor, always commanded a smile from me. At twenty-one, he was the youngest of all of my teachers, and although he'd never been anything but professional with me, my imagination ran wild anytime I saw him. That long blond hair flying in the wind as he rode his favorite horse across the field, those bright green eyes filled with joy as he looked over at me and waved. Ah yes, Aaron. My smile spread even farther as he dusted his hands off on his well-worn snug blue jeans.

"Mabel, it's a surprise to see you. It's not time for your private lesson, is it?" He paused in front of me.

"Oh no, not until tomorrow." I cleared my throat as my heart pounded. "I just wanted to introduce you to a new student at Oak Brook. This is Oliver."

Oliver thrust out his hand. "Pleasure."

"Welcome, Oliver." Aaron gave his hand a squeeze then smiled as he released it. "I'm sure you'll like it here. Oak Brook has a great reputation, with some of the best students in the country." He winked at me.

"I'm trying to convince him of that." I ignored the way my heart skipped a beat when Aaron winked at me. "He enjoys riding horses back home, so I thought maybe you could give him the riding test. I know usually you like to do a few lessons first, but since he's experienced..." I shrugged as I glanced over at Oliver as he walked over to one of the horses.

"Sure, I can set that up." Aaron pulled his phone out of his back pocket. "Let me see where I have an opening."

Oliver opened the gate to the stall and stepped inside. He stroked the horse's neck and his mane.

"What a beauty."

"That's Clover. He's not available to ride at the moment. He's still being broken-in." Aaron continued to search through his phone. "I'm a little booked up but I'm sure we can fit something in. Maybe at the end of the week?"

"Can't you fit him in today?" I frowned. "I'm sure it won't

take long. He's a great rider. I just think it might help him feel a little less homesick if he had the chance to ride."

"That's so sweet of you, Mabel." Aaron smiled at me.

"I'm not homesick." Oliver glared at me. "And I'm not waiting until the end of the week either. I can ride just fine. I've broken in horses on my own; I don't need a test to prove that I can ride."

"Those are the rules here." Aaron's shoulders tensed. "If you're not willing to follow them, then we're going to have a problem."

"No problem at all." Oliver stared hard at Aaron.

"Oliver!" I gasped as Oliver mounted the horse right inside the stall.

FOUR

"Hey, I said he's not ready to ride." Aaron's eyes flashed as he started to step in front of the stall.

Before he could, Oliver guided Clover out through the gate and down along the corridor of the stable.

"He's fine." Oliver stroked Clover's mane. "I like a little spirit in my horses." He urged the horse to go faster the moment they cleared the entrance of the stable.

"Stop!" Aaron shoved his phone back into his pocket and ran after him.

Stunned, I stared after the two for a second. Then I jumped into action. I couldn't let him get away. If he got hurt on his first day at Oak Brook, Principal Carter would certainly hold me responsible.

I led my favorite horse out of the stable and climbed up into her saddle.

"Alright, Goldie, let's catch up." I gave her golden mane a light stroke, then urged her to chase after Oliver.

As I blew past Aaron, I heard him shout my name.

"Mabel! Don't get too close to that horse! He's still wild!"

My heart pounded. If Clover was still wild that meant his

behavior would be a little unpredictable. Oliver could be thrown, or worse, trampled or kicked.

"Oliver! Stop the horse!" I encouraged Goldie to speed up.

Although I enjoyed horseback riding, I didn't consider myself an expert. I mainly took the lessons just to spend time with Aaron—and I'd learned that the more mistakes I made, the more time he spent with me.

When I glanced back over my shoulder, I noticed that Aaron had mounted Racer, a black stallion that he often rode. Within seconds he began gaining on both Oliver and me.

Oliver appeared to be perfectly content to continue his ride. As he neared the exercise ring, I saw him lean down closer to the horse. My eyes widened as I realized that he intended to jump with the horse. Could Clover even do that?

"Stop! Oliver, stop!" Aaron had nearly caught up to me, but his voice projected much farther. Even with the sound of pounding hooves all around us, Oliver had to be able to hear him.

As I watched, Oliver glanced back over his shoulder just long enough to meet my eyes, then he turned his attention back to the hurdle ahead of him. A second later, Clover launched himself into the air and easily cleared the first hurdle.

When Clover landed, Oliver let out a loud cheer and laughed.

I slowed Goldie down right beside him.

"What are you doing?" I glared at him. "You could have been hurt or even killed!"

"Oh, I thought this was the test?" He raised an eyebrow as he looked at me, then stroked his hand down along Clover's mane. "Did I pass, Aaron?" He glanced at Aaron as he finally caught up.

"Get off the horse." Aaron scowled as he slid off Racer and landed on the ground right beside Clover.

"I'll ride him back." Oliver started to turn the horse.

"Get off the horse or I'll knock you off myself." Aaron's hands balled into fists at his sides, which caused the muscles on his bare arms to stand out.

"Aaron, I think there was just a misunderstanding." I took a step toward him.

"There was no misunderstanding, was there, Oliver? Get off the horse! Now!"

"Relax, no need to overreact." Oliver slid down off the horse and offered Aaron the reins. "He likes to go fast and he likes to jump. Give him a little more time doing that and he'll be as docile as a pony."

Aaron snatched the reins from Oliver, then glared into his eyes. "You have no idea how dangerous what you just did was—not only to you, but also to Clover. You have five minutes to get off this property before I call the police. Don't even think about coming back here." He began to walk both horses back to the stable.

"Mate, don't be like that." Oliver called after him. "I just wanted a little fun. I didn't cause any harm." Oliver sighed.

"One more word!" Aaron glared over his shoulder. "And Mabel." He met my eyes. "Don't you bring him here again or you won't be welcome here either."

I felt his words like a jab to the chest. My secret crush on Aaron was one of the few guilty pleasures I allowed myself. Of course I knew there could never be anything between us, but that didn't mean I didn't enjoy the fantasy.

"I'm so sorry, Aaron, I had no idea he would act this way." I shouted after him before glaring at Oliver. "What were you thinking?"

"That I can probably ride better than that bloke." He rolled his eyes. "It's not my fault he takes himself too seriously."

"You'd better go, he's serious about calling the police." I

frowned as I started to guide Goldie to turn back toward the stables.

"Room for one more?" He launched himself up onto the horse behind me before I could answer.

"This horse isn't used to riding two people." I frowned as I looked over my shoulder at him.

He leaned forward so that our faces were only inches apart.

"It'll be fine. She's strong." He gave the horse's side a light pat. "Let's get out of here before things get messy." He stretched his arms around me and picked up the reins.

"Oliver, I can handle it." I started to take the reins back, but he snapped Goldie into action.

"Let's let her get a good sprint going." He shifted closer, his arms tightening around me, and the horse began to race beneath us.

My heart pounded, as I didn't usually ride very fast. Though I rode often, my confidence had not grown strong enough to really allow Goldie to open up to her full potential. As she galloped, I felt the wind brush against my skin and my body rocked back against Oliver's. His broad chest pressed against my back and his strong arms kept me in place on the saddle. I could barely take a breath as my emotions swam between fury and excitement. I'd never felt so free as I did in that moment, with Goldie practically flying through the air and the strange but enchanting sensation of Oliver's body wrapped around mine.

I felt his cheek brush against my skin as he leaned forward and spoke directly into my ear.

"We could just keep going if you want. All you have to do is say the word. Do you want to keep going, Maby?" He started to steer the horse toward the open field instead of the stables.

For a split-second the word "yes" burned on the tip of my tongue. A part of me never wanted to stop. The thrill of the entire experience left me speechless. But that second passed as I recalled the fury in Aaron's eyes and his warning about the police.

"No." I forced the word out, despite my desire to answer differently. "Take us back to the stables—now." I tried to grab the reins, but instead my hands curled around his.

"I'll take you back." He spoke into my ear once more, then guided the horse back toward the stable.

We were halfway there before I realized my hands were still on top of his. I pulled them away and gritted my teeth. The whole experience had been strange and completely unpredictable. I wasn't used to that. I tended to be the one in control and I preferred it that way. Things fell into place for me, and if they didn't, I always found a way to make them. But Oliver? I had no idea where he was supposed to fit.

"Last chance." He whispered in my ear as we neared the stable. "All you have to do is say it and we can break free."

"Stop it." I frowned as I shifted forward on the saddle in an attempt to escape the nearness of his lips. "I want off this horse and away from you."

FIVE

Aaron stared up at us as Goldie eased to a stop in front of him. He grabbed the reins that Oliver released.

"Your five minutes are up."

"Like I said, I caused no harm." He slid down from Goldie's back.

Oliver offered me his hand to help me down in the same moment that Aaron offered me his. For an instant I considered taking Oliver's, but instead I let Aaron's warm hand close over mine. I noticed that his grasp was rougher than usual.

"Why did you bring him here?" He tugged me down a bit quicker than I was prepared for and I stumbled forward against him.

Flustered, I took a sharp breath and looked up at him. "He's new, like I said. And I didn't know he would do anything like this."

"I could have told you." Aaron glared past me at Oliver. "Boys like that—they're bad news, Mabel." He met my eyes. "I thought you were smarter than that."

"Ease off, old man." Oliver grinned as he walked around the

horse. "I thought she could use a little fun. She seemed a little tense." His eyes shined with amusement.

"You have no idea what I need." I crossed my arms as I stared at him. How dare he act as if he knew a single thing about me?

"I was talking about the horse." He laughed and gave Goldie's back a light pat. "Horses love to run, you know. If you don't give them a chance to feel free, they'll never be content." He looked over at Aaron. "But I'm sure you know that, right? Since you're the expert?"

"Get out." Aaron pointed toward the road. "I don't want to see you here again, do you understand me?"

"I understand alright." Oliver chuckled then walked toward the road.

"Aaron, I'm really sorry." I frowned as I tried to meet his eyes.

"Sure." He guided Goldie into the stable. "Just don't bring him around here again."

"I won't, I promise." I called out to him as he disappeared into the stable. "We're still on for our private lesson, right?"

"I'll be here," Aaron called back.

As I looked back at the road, I noticed that Oliver still stood there waiting. I felt a surge of anger as I saw the faint smirk on his lips.

I marched toward him with vicious words already brewing.

"I don't know who you think you are, but I'm not going to let you come here and cause all kinds of trouble!"

"You're not going to let me?" He grinned as he held the gate open for me. "I don't recall asking for permission."

"Maybe where you're from people let this type of behavior slide, but around me, it's not going to fly." I glared at him.

"I have no interest in impressing you. You said you wanted

to show me around. And—well, this is me." He spread his arms wide. "Are you having fun yet?"

"Not even a little bit." I tried to push the memory of what I'd felt while riding Goldie with him out of my mind. It had been a complete sensation of freedom. "In fact, you're lucky that Aaron didn't knock you out."

"You Americans." He scowled at me. "So violent. I don't think your boyfriend would have dared to lay a finger on me."

"My what?" My heart skipped a beat as I stared at him. Was it that obvious?

"He's a bit old for you, don't you think?" He crossed his arms.

"Aaron is my teacher, that's all." I frowned as I walked past him, back toward the end of the road.

"We're going to have to wait for a taxi to come out now. Unbelievable." I pulled out my phone to order one.

"I'm sure he is just your teacher, but that's not all you want him to be." He jogged up beside me and then began to walk backwards in front of me as he spoke. "I saw the way you looked at him."

"You're crazy." I rolled my eyes and stepped around him as I quickened my pace.

"Am I?" He caught up with me. "I'm not the one lusting after someone out of my reach."

"I'm not lusting after anyone." I felt my cheeks grow hot and I did my best to avoid his eyes. "I don't have any plans to date anyone while I'm in high school."

"At all?" He slowed to a stop. "Are you serious?"

"Of course I'm serious." I waved down the taxi that approached. "Dating in high school is pointless and a distraction. Real love comes with maturity, something that teenagers just don't have."

"Real love can come any time." He matched my pace. "There isn't some perfect part of your life where it happens."

"There certainly is." I paused as we reached the school. "Oliver, if you want to live a reckless life, that's your choice. But I have a plan. As long as I stay focused on my education, my life isn't going to go in a great direction. High school is full of hormones, sloppy kisses, and ridiculous drama. None of that will get me to where I want to go."

"Hormones and sloppy kisses?" He quirked an eyebrow. "Sounds like you've had some bad experiences."

"Not at all. Like I said, dating is for college, not high school." I sighed as I looked at him. "I get that you're the new guy, and for whatever reason, you feel the need to cause trouble. But let me make it clear to you. Everyone here at Oak Brook has their own issues. You being a foreigner with a bad attitude doesn't make you special, it makes you just like every other hormone-ridden drama queen around here. It's my job to show you around, but I can't force you to let me. So, if you'd rather spend your time impressing the soft-minded girls around here with your fancy little bad boy streak and your sexy accent, then please, don't waste another second of my time."

"Wow." He took a step back as he stared at me. "That's quite a mouthful, isn't it?" He smiled. "I'm pretty sure you said my accent is sexy." He smirked. "Does it drive you wild when I talk?" He took a few steps toward me. "Shall I offer you a spot of tea?"

"Ugh! You're hopeless." I shook my head and pulled open the door of the taxi. As I sat down inside, Oliver sat down beside me.

"I'm just trying to help you to relax. You're so serious." He tipped his head to the side. "Maybe that's because you've never been kissed."

My cheeks heated up again and this time my anger broke through my attempt to be patient.

"That's it! My life is my business, Oliver! I don't need your help with anything. I'm doing just fine on my own, thank you." I crossed my arms as the taxi pulled out. "Just please, don't speak to me again."

"I thought you were supposed to show me around?" He scooted closer to me. "I don't want to go back so soon. You can show me around the city."

"You can hang out in the common room; I'm sure you can find someone to keep you entertained." I refused to turn back to look at him.

"Fine, I'll explore by myself." As the taxi neared the city again, Oliver pulled some cash out of his wallet. "Drop her off, then take me to the best place you can think of." He handed the driver a wad of cash.

"It doesn't work that way." I glared at him. "We have to travel in pairs. If you don't come back with me, we'll both be in trouble."

"Well then, I guess you're stuck with me." He looked over at me with a smile. "Maybe you can show me your favorite place."

I crossed my arms and scowled. "Take us to Central Park."

SIX

Sitting next to Oliver in the taxi was excruciating. He already knew too much about me. He knew about my crush on Aaron and he also knew something that I'd never told anyone.

I'd never been kissed.

My mother had instilled a deep sense of autonomy in me from a young age and warned me not to get caught up in silly romance. As a result, I'd steered clear of anything close to a boyfriend.

Once in grade school a boy had given me a flower and then tried to kiss my cheek. That was my last day at that school, and I guess that boy thought twice about ever giving another girl a flower. My mother found me another school and warned me to politely walk away from unwanted romance instead of handing out black eyes.

In the years that passed, I had to resist throwing a punch a few times, but I still managed to get my message across. I would not be caught up in the drama and chaos of young love. I'd seen far too much of it as my friends suffered through heartbreak and uncertainty. I had zero interest. But that didn't mean I wanted everyone to know how inexperienced I actually was.

So many of my friends came to me for advice. Would they still do that if they knew my secret? I had told a few white lies over time about my adventures that never happened. I didn't want to lose their trust over it.

As we stepped out of the cab at Central Park, I glanced around at the crowded sidewalks. Maybe I could just blend in and accidentally lose him. That could be forgiven, right?

He wrapped his arm around mine. "So? This is your favorite place?"

"Not even close. But if you want to spend some time in the city, this is a nice place to do it." I pulled my arm free of his. "So, have your fun, then we can go back."

"I must have really touched a sensitive spot." He met my eyes. "Or are you always this prickly?"

"I'm not prickly." I shot a glare in his direction. "I just see that you think the rules don't apply to you."

"Not exactly. It's more like, I think that rules don't exist." He shrugged. "I mean, they don't actually. They're just words written down on a piece of paper. They're not real."

"They're real enough to get me kicked out of school."

"You?" He shook his head as he grinned. "Never."

"What's that supposed to mean?"

"It means that you don't seem like the type that would ever get kicked out of school—or out of anywhere." His voice softened a little as he continued. "You're the kind of person that everyone likes."

"I wish that was the case."

"No, you don't. Trust me." He frowned. "If everyone likes you, it's because you don't really exist."

"What kind of nonsense is that?" I glared at him. "Of course I exist. You're just full of drama, aren't you?"

"Fine, stay stuck in your little world." He waved his hand through the air as he turned and walked away from me.

"We're supposed to stay together!"

"I'll text you when I'm ready to go back." He continued down the sidewalk.

I took a step toward him, then stopped. I wasn't about to follow after him like some lost puppy dog. I wasn't going to give him the satisfaction. Instead, I turned and walked the other way.

As I wandered through the streets of New York City, I realized that it was the first time that I'd explored the city alone. I'd always had a friend with me in the past. Being surrounded by strangers gave me an entirely different perspective on the city.

I felt tiny. I felt as if I could just disappear in the flood of people and no one would even notice. Was that how Oliver felt? Alone in a new place? I doubted it. Someone with his inflated ego probably didn't have a clue what loneliness was.

As I made my way back toward Central Park, I wondered if Oliver would ever text me. I guessed that he might have just decided to continue on with his day of exploring and he didn't care in the least whether I got in trouble for it.

I searched for him throughout that section of the park and finally spotted him engaged in a game of chess with an elderly man. I opened my mouth to tell him that he had to come back with me right away but stopped when I heard a snippet of his conversation.

"It's alright, take your time."

"Sometimes I can't remember." The man sighed as he stared at the pieces.

"Just relax, it'll come back to you. I'm not in any rush."

Alone in New York City with free rein to go wherever he pleased, Oliver had ended up across from a man who couldn't remember how to play chess. Why?

I stepped behind a nearby statue and continued to watch. The man's hand trembled as he picked up a piece, then set it back down without moving it.

"No, that's not it."

"Can I tell you a story?" Oliver cleared his throat.

"A story? I guess." The man frowned as he stared at the pieces.

"Once my father and I took a walk down by this pond."

"To feed the ducks?" The man picked up another piece.

"To feed the ducks." Oliver smiled. "I saw the water lap at the sand."

"Over the pebbles?" He moved the piece to a new spot on the board.

"Over the pebbles. I saw a smooth, flat pebble."

"Did you skip it?" He looked up at Oliver with a smile.

"I did." Oliver met the man's eyes. "It hopped right across the water."

"What a beautiful day." The man grinned.

"It was." Oliver raised an eyebrow. "It looks like you beat me."

"I did?" The man laughed as he looked at the board. "Well, I guess I did. Would you look at that? It's been so long since I've won a game."

"Thanks for playing." Oliver offered him his hand.

"My pleasure, young man." The man shook it, then shook his head as he looked back at the board.

Oliver stood up and started to walk away when he caught sight of me peeking around the statue.

"Spying?" He shoved his hands in his pockets.

"Waiting." I bit into my bottom lip. I wanted to ask him why he'd played with the man, but I decided against it. But as we walked back toward the street together, I couldn't resist asking him about the story he'd told.

"You and your father are close? Did you feed the ducks with him often?"

"Never." He chuckled. "My father is a businessman. He doesn't have time for things like that."

"But I heard you tell that man the story. Did you make it up?" I frowned. "Why?"

"It's a special kind of story. It helps people who are in the beginning stages of Alzheimer's. By posing familiar situations—ones that just about everyone has experienced—it gives them a chance to recall their own memories of something similar and starts them on a path of feeling confident that they can reconnect with some situations which helps them to relax." He shrugged. "Stress can make recollecting things—like how to play chess—a lot harder. So, by telling him the story, I helped him to relax and he remembered how to make the winning move."

"That's pretty amazing. How did you learn that?" I tried to meet his eyes.

"Just something I've picked up along the way." He winked at me. "I'm a fascinating fellow, you know."

I rolled my eyes as I hailed a cab for us. As much as I wanted to tell him that he wasn't, the truth was that I did find Oliver fascinating. One moment he infuriated me; the next, he left me more curious than I'd ever felt.

SEVEN

In the taxi, we kept our distance from one another. I noticed that he made an effort not to slide my way when the taxi turned. I did the same. All of the anger and frustration I'd felt toward him had been muted by the sight of him interacting with someone that most people probably overlooked.

That was unexpected.

As the taxi pulled up to Oak Brook, I felt some relief. At least being home meant that I had a way to escape him. I stepped out of the taxi, then leaned back in to pay the fare.

When I straightened up, I found Oliver right beside me.

"Are you going to turn me in now?" He stared at me, his body close enough to mine to make me wonder if he intended to touch me.

"Shouldn't I?"

"Perhaps." He hooked his thumbs into his front pockets and tipped his head enough to bring him closer to my height. "It won't make a difference to me."

"You'll have your rights to leave the campus revoked." I searched his eyes. "Won't that matter?"

"My rights to leave the campus?" He narrowed his eyes. "Am I a prisoner now?"

"It just shows that you can't be trusted. It's Oak Brook's job to keep all of its students safe. That includes you."

"Not for long." He shrugged. "Besides, like I said—"

"Rules don't exist. Yes, I heard you." I sighed as I studied him. "Oliver, you disappoint me."

"Pardon?" He quirked an eyebrow.

"I've been bored. So bored. For a long time now. I've been hoping that something interesting would happen, something that would break up the monotony that has become my life. When I heard you were coming, I thought maybe this was it. Maybe this new student from an entirely different continent would have something new to teach me, something eye-opening to share. But here you are, just as sullen and broken as the rest of the ultra-privileged students at this school."

"Wow, I've heard rumors that you can be pretty judgmental, but this is a whole new level." He ran his hand across the curve of his chin as he smiled. "Is it exhausting to be so self-righteous?"

"Whatever." I shoved past him, through the entrance to Oak Brook. I didn't want to look at him—not for a single second longer. In fact, I hoped that I wouldn't have to see him again.

As I stalked toward the dormitories, I didn't dare look back over my shoulder. I didn't want to think about him following after me or smirking behind my back. I didn't want to hear his words echo through my mind.

Someone told him I was judgmental? So what? Why would that bother me? Everyone knew that I could be a little judgmental. So why did it make me feel so much more vulnerable when he said it?

I burst through the door of my dorm room and marched right into the kitchen.

"Maby?" Fifi pulled the earbuds from her ears and stood up from the sofa. "Are you okay?"

"I don't want to talk about it. I need a drink." I slammed a half-gallon of milk down on the kitchen counter and grabbed a glass.

"What's going on?" She walked up to the counter that separated the kitchenette from the living room.

"Fi, didn't you hear me?" I poured some milk into a glass, then grabbed a packet of chocolate powder from the box I kept on the top shelf of the cabinet above the sink.

"I heard you, that doesn't mean I believe you. You clearly need to talk about something." She leaned back against the counter beside me. "Let me guess. That something's name is Oliver? I heard you took off with him this morning."

"Nope, nope." I snapped my fingers as I spoke. "His name is not to be spoken here, understand me?"

"Seriously?" Fifi laughed, but her smile faded as I glared at her. "You're serious. Okay." She held up her hands. "The unnamed seems to have gotten under your skin."

"I don't even want to think about him. I just want to have some dinner and have a nice night. Okay?" I stirred my chocolate milk so violently that a bit of the milk swirled up over the rim of the glass.

"I think it's mixed." Fifi took the spoon from my hand. "Whatever he did, Maby, don't let him get to you. You're a great person and if he has you this upset, that just shows what a jerk he is."

"Thanks, Fi." I smiled, then took a long swallow of the chocolate milk. The sweet silky substance soothed me to some degree, but I couldn't help wondering if she was right.

Was he a jerk or did he just talk to me in ways no one else dared to? I'd worked hard at creating a confident and untouchable persona, but he acted as if it didn't even exist, as if he could see right through it. Was it just arrogance on his part or did he see further than anyone ever had?

I finished my chocolate milk, then turned to Fifi.

"Ready to go to dinner? I could use some time around some decent people."

"Sure. Let me just grab my phone." She walked off toward her room.

As I watched Fifi step through the door, I remembered another person going into that room. Someone who actually knew me better than anyone else on earth. A friend that I hadn't heard from in far too long.

I pulled out my own phone and flipped to Jennifer's number. It didn't work anymore. She'd changed it. Or maybe someone else had. Either way, I couldn't reach her. But her picture was still there, with that smile that never quit. She'd know exactly what to tell me about Oliver. She'd help me figure it all out.

"Ready?" Fifi paused beside me.

I turned off my phone before she could see the picture.

"Yes. Please. I need some cheesy nachos."

"Mm, that sounds good! We'd better hurry before they're all gone." Fifi rushed through the door with me right behind her. I was glad to have her as a friend, as I was glad to have all my friends, but none of them were quite the friend that I'd had in Jennifer. We'd been more like sisters. But sisters didn't just disappear.

At our usual table in the cafeteria, surrounded by my friends, I began to relax. I could patch things up with Aaron; that wouldn't be a problem. I just had to put the bad day behind me and focus on the future as I always did.

One day I'd be far from Oak Brook Academy—far from teenage drama and hormones—in a new place where my life would finally have a chance to begin. As I lost myself in a fantasy of bumping into Aaron when I was in my twenties, I heard the sharp snap of a tray being set down on the table.

"Mind if I join?"

That voice. That accent. Oh no.

"Sure." Alana patted the table. "There's always room for one more."

I looked up just as Oliver sat down across from me.

"Oh, cheesy nachos. Great, they were all out." He reached over and grabbed a cheese-laden tortilla chip from my plate. "Kind of you to offer." He flashed me a smile.

I resisted the urge to smack the chip out of his hand and forced a smile. "I didn't offer. But please, take what you want. I've lost my appetite anyway."

EIGHT

I noticed the shocked look on my friends' faces as they all turned their attention to me.

I was never one to turn down food. In fact, I often finished up whatever they had left.

As I stared across the table at Oliver, I felt his eyes bore into mine.

"Pardon, did I overstep?" He popped the chip into his mouth.

The crunch carried loudly across the mostly quiet table as all eyes remained on me.

"Not at all. I'd like you to have everything you want, Oliver." I slid the tray toward him.

"No thanks." He pushed the tray back toward me. "I just wanted one."

"I doubt that." I nudged the tray back in his direction. "You don't seem the type to stop after just one bite."

"I am." He pushed the tray back.

"If neither of you want them, I'll take them!" Wes grinned as he reached for the tray.

"Don't!" I smacked his hand sharply.

"Ouch!" He glared at me.

"Harsh." Oliver quirked an eyebrow. "I think you'd better eat those chips. You seem a little hangry."

"Enough." Candy rolled her eyes. "I don't know what is going on between the two of you, but this is ridiculous." She looked over at me.

"Everything's fine, Candy." I met her eyes. Of all my friends, Candy was the most sensitive. She hid it well, but it really bothered her whenever there was disharmony or drama. "Oliver's right, I probably am a little hangry." I plucked a chip from the plate and popped it into my mouth.

The others seemed to take this as a symbol that everything was fine.

As the conversation picked back up, I watched the way that Oliver interacted with my friends. He flashed smiles, told stories about his life in England, and even cracked a few jokes with Chuckles, the clown of our little ensemble of friends. He certainly didn't lack an ounce of charm when it came to my friends, but each time his gaze shifted back to me, his smile faded.

Had I offended him so deeply that he couldn't stand the sight of me?

It was probably for the best. I finished the last of my food, then stood up.

"Good night all, see you in the morning." As I started to leave the table, Apple caught my hand and held onto it.

"Where are you going? Aren't we going to hang out tonight?" She met my eyes.

I knew what she meant. She wanted to meet up in the hideout like we always did. It was a building we'd discovered in an area of the campus that was no longer used for classes. Instead, the buildings were used for storage and we'd taken over one in particular to be our home away from home. It was a sacred place.

"Not tonight. I'm a little tired." I glanced briefly at Oliver, then looked back at Apple. "Besides, we have choir tomorrow."

"Choir?" Oliver's eyes widened as he smiled. "I didn't peg you for a church -going girl."

"It's not that kind of choir." Apple grinned. "You should come, I'll bet you'd like it."

"He didn't get permission." I narrowed my eyes.

"Don't worry, I can arrange it." Apple looked over at Oliver. "Trust me, just be ready to leave by eight. It'll be worth it."

"I wouldn't miss it." He smiled as he met my eyes. "See you in the morning, Maby."

I managed to resist glaring at him. To all my friends he was a charming new student. I didn't want them to think I was cruel. But I sensed the darkness behind his smile.

He didn't want to go with us for any other reason than to torture me.

"Fine." I gritted my teeth as I turned and walked away.

I'd have a short time without him, long enough for me to reset my attitude and get him out from under my skin. At least that's what I thought before I felt a hand wrap around my wrist just as I reached the hallway.

I turned quickly to find Oliver right behind me.

"Wait, can I talk to you?"

"Why?" I tore my hand from his grasp. "What could you possibly have to say to me?"

"I know things got off to a rough start between us." He met my eyes. "I shouldn't have acted the way I did."

"Is this some kind of joke?"

"It's not a joke." He swept his hands back across his hair and sighed. "I'm still getting used to being here, okay? It isn't exactly by choice."

"What do you mean?" I studied him. "You were forced to come here?"

"In a way, yes. It wasn't my idea." He shook his head. "I've got a lot going on right now. But I shouldn't have taken it out on you."

"No, you shouldn't have." I crossed my arms. "But I'm not sure if I believe any of this. You've spent the day trying to pluck every nerve I have, and now all of a sudden you have a change of heart?"

"It's not a change of heart." He frowned and took a slight step back. "I'm just trying to minimize the damage I cause."

"It's not working." I met his eyes. "You're not very good at apologies."

"Apologies aren't worth anything, are they?" He lowered his voice as he spoke, then took a step in my direction. "Is that what you want me to say? I'm sorry?" He searched my eyes. "Will that make you believe me?"

"No." I frowned as I stared back at him. Despite how irritated I was, the moment we made eye contact, I felt as if he drew me in. I felt an irresistible urge to see as far as I possibly could. "Why don't you just try telling me the truth? What are you so upset about?"

"Never mind that." He smiled and I watched his charm resurface, like a mask he could easily put on and take off as it suited him. "I'll see you in the morning, right?"

"I guess I don't have much choice, do I?" I shook my head. "Hopefully you can handle it." As I turned and walked away, I bit into the tip of my tongue.

I wanted to say a lot more. I wanted to tell him that he should just go back to England if he didn't want to be here. I wanted to insist that he not go with us the next morning. But there was no point. He would do what he wanted to do—whatever pleased him—and nothing I could say would stop him.

After a fitful night's sleep, I woke up with a pressure in my chest, almost as if I couldn't breathe. Was it nerves about singing?

I rubbed my hand along my throat and took a slow breath. My lungs filled just fine, but the pressure remained. I took another breath and pressed my hand against my chest. The moment that my hand settled over my heart, Oliver's face flashed through my mind. My stomach jolted and I took a sharp breath.

"No, no, no!" I jumped out of bed and rushed over to the mirror on my vanity. As I stared into my own eyes, I spoke in a firm tone. "No way, Mabel, do you hear me? Not a chance. Get it out of your head right this second because it's not going to happen!"

I felt my heartbeat quicken with my hand still pressed against my chest. I closed my eyes tight and tried to imagine Aaron instead. Aaron with his hair flowing in the wind as he rode his horse.

For a moment, I did see Aaron, but a second later it was Oliver mounting Clover despite Aaron's protests.

"Ugh!" I flopped back against my bed and groaned. How could this be happening?

NINE

When my phone rang, I tried to ignore it. The last thing I wanted to do was end up in New York City with Oliver again. But a few minutes later I heard pounding on the dorm room door.

"Maby!" Fi called out from her bedroom. "I know it's not for me!"

I sighed as I pushed myself up out of bed. There'd been a time when I'd looked forward to choir. It had been my favorite thing to do. Now, it felt more like a chore.

I could already hear Oliver's comments when he saw me on stage. His sharp tongue would have a lot of exercise.

"I'm on my way, Candy!" I gathered my dress and a few things I needed for my hair and my make-up and shoved it all in the usual bag. As I pulled on a pair of jeans and tossed on a blouse, I tried to remember the excitement I'd once felt.

Jennifer and I would sing as we got ready. We'd dance our way to the bus stop. Everything was better then. I could hear her voicing her opinion about Oliver.

"You've got a crush on that English boy!" she would sing into her hairbrush. She'd dance around me in circles and laugh so loud that she'd wake up the girls in the next dorm. She would make even my misery fun.

"It's about time." Candy sighed as I stepped out the door into the hall.

"Sorry, I overslept." I shrugged.

"Really?" She cupped my chin and looked at my face. "Because it looks like you didn't sleep at all."

"I've been having a rough time lately, that's all." I frowned as I followed her down the hallway. "I'm just a little out of sorts."

"You're not the only one, trust me. With everyone hooking up lately, it's hard not to feel like I'm the odd one out." She tiptoed through the commons, then pushed the door open to the courtyard.

Someone outside pulled the door out of her hands and held it open for both of us.

Candy stepped out ahead of me.

I paused when I saw who held the door.

Oliver. Oliver, who'd shown up in my fantasy this morning. Oliver, who most certainly didn't belong there.

"Morning, sunshine." He smiled at me.

"Chipper in the morning, aren't you?" I stepped past him and greeted Apple with a hug.

"I made sure he was up and ready to go. I don't want him to miss a minute." Apple laughed.

"Does that mean you're going to perform a solo today?" I met her eyes.

"No way." She drew back. "Not happening, you know that."

"One of these days." I winked at her. Apple's shyness was something I'd been trying to break her out of, but it wasn't the easiest thing to do.

"Now I'm even more curious. Are we waiting for anyone else?" Oliver fell into step with the group.

"No, this is it. A few other girls used to sing, but various activities took over their time." Candy looped her arm through Oliver's.

I noticed that he didn't pull away. I also noticed that Candy made sure her head brushed briefly against his shoulder.

A hint of relief allowed me to take a deep breath. Maybe Candy would pair up with Oliver and I could stop thinking about him once and for all.

On the bus, he sat beside Candy and I settled into a seat of my own. As I watched the sun spill across the high-rise buildings, I remembered the feeling of being alone in the middle of the city. It still sent a small shiver up my spine. I pushed the thought from my mind.

I wasn't alone. I had friends that cared about me, a mother who adored me, and a future that couldn't be any more bright. Why would I dwell on a few minutes of loneliness during a very strange day?

We piled off the bus and headed into the small theater. It was about as familiar to me as my own dorm room. I'd been part of the choir since I'd started at Oak Brook as a freshman and I hoped to continue until my very last day.

"You're going to love this, Oliver. Make sure you get a good seat." Candy blew him a kiss, then grabbed my hand and tugged me behind the stage. "One more second of that accent and I might just turn into a puddle." She laughed.

"Really? I find it a little annoying." I scrunched up my nose as I pulled on my dress, then added a few props to my costume.

"How is that even possible?" She frowned as she looked at me. "It doesn't matter, anyway. He's clearly not into me. He keeps asking me questions about you."

"Me?" I stared back at her.

"Yes, you. It's pretty obvious he has a thing for you." She tugged on a long red wig.

"No offense, Candy, but you don't have a clue. He can barely stand being around me." I turned my back to her. "Can you zip me?"

"Have I mentioned that I love this dress on you?" She pulled up the zipper. "If he isn't into you yet, when he sees you in this, he's going to be head over heels."

"I doubt it. But I suspect he has a thing for redheads." I smiled as I turned to face her. "You should go out there and work it."

"Oh, are you pushing me his way?" She narrowed her eyes. "What's that about? Why not try things out and see what happens?"

"You know my rule, Candy. No dating in high school. Besides, he doesn't want anything to do with me and I want even less to do with him. So please, just drop it."

"If you say so." She shrugged. "But I know what I see when I see it."

I held back my opinion. I didn't want to cause any more drama than I already faced with Oliver in the audience.

As we paraded on stage, the music blasted and the crowd cheered. It had gotten larger over the years. It was still only about fifty people or so, but it was a fun way to spend our Sunday mornings.

As we began to sing our ridiculous songs in our ridiculous costumes, I felt a particular pair of eyes on me.

"All we have to do is shake, shake, shake!" Candy sang out, then turned around and thrust her bottom out to the audience. As she shook it beneath her fluffy skirt, the audience cheered. Apple was the next to spin around and shake and as they continued down the line, I wondered if I should just skip it. But I didn't want to ruin the show. I certainly didn't want to let Oliver's presence stop me from being exactly who I was.

When it was my turn, I spun around and shook it just as enthusiastically as I always did.

When I turned back around, I looked out into the audience and noticed the shocked look on his face. It made me smile wider than I had in a long time. He applauded along with the rest of the audience.

After we changed, I stepped out of the dressing room to find him in the hallway.

"Well, that was a strange parade you all put on." He chuckled as he held the door for me.

"Didn't you like it?" I batted my eyes at him.

"Oh, I liked it just fine. I can't say I understand it, though. Why would you want to be part of such a display?"

"If you'd listened to the lyrics, you would know. It's meant to ridicule society's view of women and their roles."

"So you are defying society's portrayal of women by dressing up and shaking your butt?"

"I wouldn't expect you to understand." I rolled my eyes as I walked toward the stairs that led to the girls' dressing room. "Did you at least enjoy yourself?" I glanced back at him.

"How could I not?" He stared at me, his lips quirked into the faintest smile. "Would you like to show me again?"

"No thanks." I turned and walked away.

Part of me expected him to follow. When he didn't, I glanced back and saw him with his phone to his ear. Too curious not to listen in, I crept closer. With his back to me, I doubted that he knew I was there.

"Shauna, I'm asking for another chance. I deserve at least that." His voice wavered, without a hint of the charm that usually oozed from him. "Please, can't you give me that?" He took a sharp breath. "Don't hang up!" He cursed under his breath as he shoved his phone into his pocket and spun around suddenly.

Startled, I ducked back against the wall hoping that the shadows in the hallway would hide me.

"Did you enjoy the show?" He glared at me.

"I just wanted to make sure you knew the way out." My cheeks flushed as I heard how lame my excuse sounded.

"No, you just wanted to be nosy." He brushed past me and headed down the hallway. As he joined the others, he gave a resounding laugh, then shot a look back at me.

I froze as he stared at me. How could I defend myself when he was right? I'd judged him so harshly, but it was beginning to become clear to me that Oliver didn't have the perfect life he portrayed.

TEN

"So, did you like it?" Candy grinned as she looped her arm around Oliver's. "Was it fantastic or what?"

"It was eye-opening." He grinned and tightened his arm around hers.

"I'll get us a taxi." I waved my hand through the air.

"So soon?" Oliver frowned. "It's a beautiful day."

"He's right." Apple nodded as she looked up at the sky. "Not too hot, nice and clear."

"We do have another hour or so before we're supposed to be back." Candy shrugged. "We could go grab some coffee or something."

"Or take him to Maby's favorite place!" Apple clapped her hands. "I bet it will shock him!"

"No, I don't think that's such a good idea." I frowned.

"Why?" Oliver looked over at me. "I'd love to see it. I tried to get her to take me yesterday, but she wouldn't."

"Really?" Candy frowned. "Why not? You showed all of us."

"It's not my favorite place anymore. Not really." I brushed

my hair back over my shoulders. "I think it's better if we just head back."

"Is she always so cheerful?" Oliver leaned closer to Candy. "Or is she just being extra sunny because I'm here?"

"Maby, are you okay?" Apple looked into my eyes.

"I'm fine. I'm just a little tired. I didn't sleep well." I rubbed my hand along the back of my neck and did my best to avoid Oliver's gaze.

"I thought you said you slept in?" Candy raised an eyebrow. "I say we take him. Even if it's not your favorite place anymore, it's still a great place to visit and he's probably never even heard of it."

"It's decided then." Oliver smiled. "I'm at your mercy, ladies."

"I like the sound of that." Candy squeezed his arm. "Let's go, Maby, it'll be great."

"Fine." I rolled my eyes, then followed after them.

It wasn't my favorite place. Not anymore. Not after everything that had changed in my life. But it was still a fun place to visit.

I followed them as we entered Grand Central Terminal and listened to their chatter as we blended with the crowd of travelers.

"Are you going to tell me where we're going?" Oliver peered over his shoulder at me.

"It's not much further." Candy laughed as she pulled him toward an oyster restaurant in the busy station.

"Wait, this is your favorite place?" He laughed as he pulled away from Candy. "I have to say that surprises me a little."

"Not the restaurant, silly." Candy huffed, then gave him a light push toward the corner.

"Wait, who's going to be on the other side?" Apple cringed. "Was I not supposed to say that?"

"Maby, go on the other side." Candy tipped her head to the other corner of the archway, across a crowd of people.

"No, you should go, Candy." I smiled as I thought about the many things she might have already thought of to say.

"Are you sure?" She locked her eyes to mine.

"Absolutely."

"I'll go with you!" Apple followed along behind Candy.

"Any excuse to be alone with me?" Oliver pursed his lips.

"Still pouring on the charm, are you?" I guided him toward the corner. "I thought me being nosy might change that."

"I'm sorry about that, I just got a little frustrated. It was personal."

"I could tell." I met his eyes briefly, then placed my hand against his head. "You have to put your ear up against the wall—where the tiles meet."

"Why?" He frowned as he drew back from my touch. "Is this some kind of prank?"

"Not at all." I pushed his head with a little more force this time but was careful not to actually knock it against the wall. "Just listen."

As my fingers lingered in the smooth silk of his hair, my chest grew tight, my head swam, and I felt the same sensation that I'd felt that morning.

"This is some kind of game." He narrowed his eyes. "Real mature."

"Sh!" Without thinking I pressed my fingertips against his lips to silence him. The jolt of electricity that raced through me took my breath away in the same moment that he caught my hand by the wrist.

For a second, it seemed as if we were both frozen. Then a strange smile spread across his lips.

"Is that Candy?" His eyes widened as he released my hand.

"I can hear her. Just like she's right next to me. How is that possible when there's a crowd of people between us?"

"It's the design of the tiles and the archway." I leaned back against the wall and looked up at the domed ceiling. "It creates a perfect place to tell secrets."

"And this is your favorite place?" He looked over at me, while keeping his ear pressed against the wall.

"It was." I shrugged. "I like the idea of being in a crowded place full of strangers and yet you can confess your most secret desires to someone on the other side of all the chaos."

"Is that why it's not your favorite place anymore?" He sought my eyes. "Because someone confessed something?"

"Now who's being nosy?" I avoided his gaze and straightened up. "You know, she's waiting for you to say something back."

"Oh." He drew his head away from the wall. "How do I do that?"

"Just put your lips up close and whisper." I shrugged.

"Could you show me?" He stepped to the side.

"She wants to hear your voice." I crossed my arms as I watched him.

"Is that because she thinks my accent is sexy?" He shifted closer to me along the wall. "Wait, wasn't that you?"

"Would you just say something?" I gave him a solid push back toward the corner.

"Violent." He made a surprised face, then leaned into the wall and whispered.

I leaned close but couldn't hear his words. "What did you say?" I met his eyes.

"That's for me and Candy to know." He stared at me. "I know you didn't want me to come here, Maby. I know that something happened here, something that not even your closest friends know about." He frowned. "I know I haven't given you a good reason to consider me a friend, but if you need somebody to talk to about it, I'm here."

"Oh?" I laughed. "Thanks, I'll keep that in mind."

"I'm serious." He took my hand just as Candy shouted from the other side of the corridor.

"Are you even listening?"

"Why don't you tell me about Shauna first?" I locked my eyes to his.

"I don't have anything to say about her." He released my hand and put his ear up against the wall again.

As I watched his cheeks fill with color, I couldn't help but wonder what Candy had whispered to him.

On our way back to Oak Brook, I sat on the opposite side of the taxi. Candy sat beside Oliver and chatted with him the entire way. I kept my eyes on the window, but my thoughts returned to the sensation I'd felt the moment I'd touched his lips. Why had I done that? Why didn't I just keep my hands to myself?

When the taxi pulled up to Oak Brook Academy, I dared to look in Oliver's direction.

Instantly his eyes met mine. Had he been watching me for some time?

He held the door open for everyone to get out.

As Apple and Candy led the way through the entrance, Oliver hung back to walk beside me.

"Thanks for sharing that with me today. I had no idea anything like that existed."

"There are a lot of things you can discover about our city, Oak Brook, and the people here if you keep an open mind." I headed in the direction of the dormitories. "I hope you find something to hold your interest." I quickened my pace and hoped that he'd take the hint that the conversation was over.

His footsteps right behind me made it clear that he didn't.

"I thought you were going to be the one to show me around?"

"I think I've shown you enough." I climbed the steps to the door of the commons and pulled it open. "You got around the city on your own just fine yesterday. I'm sure you'll be good."

He stepped into the commons behind me. "But why? Is it because of what I said about Shauna?"

"It doesn't matter, does it? I'm sure you can have more fun with someone else." I started up the stairs to the girls' dormitory.

"Fine. If that's what you want." He shoved his hands into his pockets and turned back toward the door.

"I'm sorry, you know." I held his gaze.

"For what?" He took a few steps toward me and paused at the bottom of the stairs.

"For whatever she did to you. I'm sure you didn't deserve it." My heart softened as I noticed the hurt surface in his eyes.

"You don't know anything about me, Maby. Not a thing. I'm going to tell you one thing that is very important for you to understand. Stay out of my business. Got it?"

I stared at him as he turned and walked away.

Just when I thought there might be a decent person beyond that charming mask, just when I thought maybe he had a heart, he made it clear that he didn't—at least not one I wanted to get to know.

I headed up the stairs. My decision was made.

In the morning, I would talk to the principal.

ELEVEN

I woke up the next morning with a heavy feeling in the pit of my stomach. After the way Oliver had spoken to me the day before, I knew he wasn't someone I wanted to be around. Yet there was still a subtle tug in the back of my mind that tried to keep me from getting out of bed—from heading to the principal's office.

Still, I ended up there.

As I sat outside his door, I rehearsed in my mind exactly what I would say. Although I was grateful for his trust, I was not the right person for this particular job. Principal Carter had to understand that, didn't he? I fiddled with my phone as I continued to wait.

In the process of swiping through apps, a particular picture surfaced. Jennifer and me, with our arms around one another, my smile as bright as hers.

Had it happened yet? I closed my eyes and did the math in my mind. Yes, it had to have happened.

"Mabel?" Principal Carter opened the door and poked his head out through it. "Sorry for the wait, I didn't expect to see you today. Please, come in." He took a step back from the door.

I drew a deep breath, then followed him into the office. How would he react? Would he be disappointed in me?

"Thanks for seeing me." I sat down in a chair in front of his desk as he sat down behind it.

"Of course, any time." He looked across the desk at me. "It sounded a bit urgent. Is everything okay?"

"Yes, everything's fine. It's just—I think it would be better if you found someone else to show the new student—to show Oliver around."

"Oh?" He frowned. "I thought you two were a perfect match. Did something happen?"

"No, not really." I held back a barrage of reasons why I never wanted to deal with Oliver again. "It's just that I have a lot on my plate this year and I thought I could take on this as well with no problem, but it turns out I can't. I can't risk my grades suffering."

"I understand. That's perfectly reasonable." He tapped a fingertip lightly against the top of his desk. "But I'm not sure that it's honest."

"Sir?" I squirmed in my chair as he continued to study me.

"It's important to me that you know you can come to me with any concerns you might have, Mabel. If there's something going on that is making you uncomfortable, I want to know about it." He looked into my eyes. "Did Oliver do something to upset you? It's not like you to shirk any kind of responsibility, and you're never going to convince me that you're concerned about your grades."

"I just don't think I'm the right person, that's all." I frowned. "Maybe Candy would be a better option? She has a lot of free time right now."

"Okay, give me a second." He picked up his phone. "Yes, please have Oliver come to my office."

"Wait, why?" I sat forward in my chair. "I said he didn't do anything wrong." My heart began to race.

"I know that." He hung up the phone and looked back at me. "But I think it would be a good idea to let him know what's going on. With him being new to our school, I wouldn't want to blindside him with a new host without some kind of explanation. You don't mind telling him yourself, do you?"

"You can't be serious." I narrowed my eyes.

"If there was no issue between you, then there shouldn't be an issue with telling him that you'd like him to have a new host, should there?" He glanced up as the office door swung open and Oliver stepped inside.

"Oliver, please, join us." He smiled as he gestured to the empty chair beside mine.

"What is this about?" Oliver sank down into the chair but avoided looking at me.

"I just wanted to let you know that I'm going to assign you a new host to help you get settled here at Oak Brook." Principal Carter smiled. "Candace. You've met her, right?"

"Yes." Oliver looked up at him. "Why?" He stole a swift glance at me, then looked back at the principal.

"Mabel?" Principal Carter met my eyes.

Stunned, I could barely take a breath. I hadn't anticipated having to tell Oliver to his face. But I wouldn't let it stop me.

"I have a lot on my plate right now, Oliver, and I think Candy would be a great host for you. I'm sure she will have plenty to show you."

"Whatever you say." He shrugged. "Is that it?" He looked back at the principal. "Can I go now?"

"I just wanted to make sure that everything is going smoothly so far, Oliver. If you have any questions or need anything at all, please know that my door is always open." He offered his hand to Oliver.

"Thanks." Oliver gave it a quick shake, then stood up from his chair and left the office. Not once did he look in my direction. My hands broke into a sweat as I realized what I'd done. I'd severed any ties we had. That was supposed to be what I wanted but watching him walk away made my mind spin into panic.

"Thanks, Mabel." Principal Carter offered me his hand as well. "I appreciate you taking the time to introduce Oliver to our school. I hope it wasn't too taxing on you."

I wiped my hand on my pants, then shook his hand.

"You're welcome." I mumbled my words, uncertain what else to say.

My heart sunk as I stepped out of the office and continued through the exterior office out into the hall. Had I been too hasty? The first class of the day had already started, which left the hall fairly empty. As I wandered along it, I was reminded of how I'd felt walking through New York City completely alone. Why did these thoughts surface now? Why did he have such an impact on me? Before Oliver showed up, I was perfectly fine with being alone. Now I felt his absence.

"So that's it then?"

His voice caused me to jump and turn to face him.

"Are you following me?" I glared at him.

"It's a hallway." He glanced over his shoulder, then back at me. "There's nowhere else for me to go."

"I just thought you'd already gone to class." I frowned.

"I don't want Candy showing me around." He met my eyes.

"Why? She's a lot of fun. She's a nice person." I shrugged.

"I'm sure she is. But she's not you."

"So?" I raised an eyebrow. "You made it pretty clear last night that you wanted me to mind my own business. That's what I'm trying to do."

"I shouldn't have talked to you like that." He leaned back against the wall and stared at me. "I'm sorry, okay?"

"Okay." I met his eyes for a second, then looked away. "I just think it's better for both of us if you have a different host."

"Do you?" He straightened up. "Why? Because I don't buy your untouchable act?"

"Oliver, you said yourself that you don't plan on being here long—that you didn't want to be here in the first place. Why does it bother you if I don't want to be your host?"

"You're the one bright spot." He sighed as he walked toward me. "You're interesting, you make me curious."

"There's nothing to be curious about." I watched him as he stopped in front of me. "I'll just be another disappointment to you, trust me."

"I doubt that." He chewed on the side of his lip, then released it as he leaned a little closer to me. "You don't have to be my host, Maby—that's your choice—but you're not going to get rid of me that easily."

"It's a free school, right?" I narrowed my eyes as my heart pounded. I absolutely despised the way he could inspire anger and desire in me in the same exact moment. How was I supposed to make sense of that? "Good luck with everything, Oliver."

I turned and walked off down the hall.

TWELVE

I made it through the first few classes of my day with my resolve intact. I just needed to create space between us. Once I accomplished that, whatever weird crush I'd managed to form on Oliver would fade.

But at lunch, as I walked into the cafeteria, I felt a rush of anticipation. He'd be at the table, wouldn't he?

I collected my food, then walked over to the table my friends and I always shared. I saw the usual crowd, but no sign of Oliver.

"Hey." I smiled as I sat down across from Candy. "How's your day going?"

"Other than getting a surprise assignment to host Oliver?" She eyed me.

"I didn't think you'd mind. Do you?" I opened my bottle of water.

"No. Well, at least I wouldn't, if I could find him." She sighed. "I waited outside all of his classes this morning and somehow he's managed to slip past me each time. I'm starting to think he's avoiding me.

JILLIAN ADAMS

"Starting to?" Apple quirked an eyebrow. "I think that message is pretty clear."

"No one asked you." Candy frowned as she crossed her arms. "I don't know why he would be avoiding me. I thought we had a nice day yesterday."

"It might be for the best." I cringed. "I'm not so sure pawning him off on you was a good idea. He's not your average guy, Candy. He has some issues." I lowered my voice as I leaned closer to her. "Maybe you should be careful."

"Careful?" She frowned. "Not all of us are holding out until college, Maby. I've been careful. Being careful has made me miss so many chances. Now, if you want to call dibs, I'll back off, but otherwise, Oliver's all mine."

"Go right ahead." I bit into my bottom lip as I did my best to ignore a wave of jealousy. What was wrong with me? How could I feel this way about a boy I barely knew, who hadn't exactly given the greatest first impression? "I think I'm going to eat in the courtyard. It's so nice out today."

I smiled at everyone at the table, then carried my tray toward the door that led out of the cafeteria and into the courtyard. As I reached it, Oliver pushed it open from the outside. He held the door for me as I stepped through.

"Are you lost? The cafeteria's the other way. Or, let me guess..." He turned to face me as I reached the other side of the doorway. "You're trying to avoid me."

"I'm not doing a very good job of it, am I?" I shrugged, despite the way my heart slammed against my chest as his eyes settled on mine.

"It doesn't have to be like this, Maby. I apologized, didn't I?"

"That was very noble of you." I nodded. "But don't flatter yourself. I like my peace and quiet now and then. Trust me, you'll have plenty of company." As I walked over to one of the stone tables in the courtyard, I willed myself not to look back. I

68

didn't want to know if he still had his eyes on me, or if he had already gone inside the cafeteria. I didn't want to know how I would feel if I looked back and saw him walking toward me. I didn't want any of it to be real.

But the moment I sat down, my head swiveled and there he was, still in the doorway, his eyes locked to me, his lips curved into a strange expression. The moment I spotted him, he let the door fall closed and disappeared into the cafeteria.

I set my tray down on the stone table and slouched down on one of the benches. As the weight of this new reality settled around me, I had to face the truth. Yes, I had developed some kind of thing for Oliver. I had fallen into some kind of love-hate trap with him and I needed to get free of it.

As I picked at my food, I recalled the man he'd played chess with and the way Oliver had transformed from arrogant and sarcastic into a caring and patient person.

Which one was the real him?

I heard the subtle thunk of a tray hitting the stone table before I looked up to see Oliver sit down across from me.

I opened my mouth to speak, but he held up one hand to stop me.

"Not a word. I'm here to eat my food in peace."

"Seriously?"

"That's a word." He narrowed his eyes.

"Fine, I'll go." I picked up my tray.

"Sit down." He met my eyes as I started to turn away.

"Excuse me?" I laughed. "Do you really think you can tell me what to do? An accent only gets you so far, buddy."

"Sit down, please." He cleared his throat. "I mean, please, will you have lunch with me?"

"Why?" I hovered near the table. My instincts told me to bolt, but I was too curious to obey them.

"Because, out of all of the people I've met, you're the only one that I want to spend time with. So please, I'd rather not be alone." He pushed his tray toward me. "I got some extra cheesy nachos."

I began to sit back down before I even realized I'd decided to stay. As I plucked a nacho from his tray, I looked into his eyes.

"I can't figure you out, Ollie."

"Ollie?" He chuckled. "That's not happening. It's Oliver."

"See? One minute you're so casual, the next you're so sensitive." I quirked an eyebrow. "Why don't you tell me what's on your mind, Ollie?"

"Stop." He frowned as he stared back at me.

"Stop what? I thought you liked spending time with me."

"I do. Sometimes." He sighed, then shook his head. "Do you even realize how infuriating you are?"

"Me?" I laughed. "That's funny coming from you."

"What are you trying to say?"

"I have never, ever, had as much trouble figuring someone out as I do you." I rested my chin on my hand and stared at him. "What are you hiding behind those beautiful eyes?"

"Sexy accent and now I have beautiful eyes too, huh?" He smirked. "I'm winning you over, you know it."

"You're avoiding the question, I know it." I stole another nacho from his plate.

"Can't I just be?" He shrugged. "Why do you need to figure me out? You don't have to pin everyone under your thumb, you know."

"I don't do that."

"Sure you do. The way your friends all look to you for permission, as if you're the expert on everything. That's because you've got them right where you want them, tucked safely under that super strong thumb of yours." He poked at the top of my thumb. "Too scared to set them free, I'd guess."

"Now who is trying to figure out who?" I smiled. "I guess we're not so different."

"No, I don't think we are." He gnawed at his bottom lip for a second, then sighed. "I really did just come out here to spend some time with you, not to cause you any trouble."

"I could leave if I wanted to. But I'm still here."

"Why?"

The question caught me off guard. I stared at him as I considered my answer. Why was I still there? What was it about him that had me so tethered to him?

"Tell me about the man in the park. The one that you helped to play chess."

"That doesn't answer my question." He frowned.

"No, it doesn't." I took a bite of my own food and waited.

"What do you want to know?" He looked into my eyes.

"You said you picked it up along the way. How?"

"Fine. My grandfather had it. He had Alzheimer's. I did what I could to help him. Is that what you want to know?" He rested his elbows on the table and leaned toward me. "Or did you want to dig a little deeper?"

"I'm sorry about your grandfather." I studied him as I imagined him doting on his grandfather. What was not to like about that?

"Now, it's your turn. Answer my question. Why are you still here? You refuse to be my host, you push me toward Candy, but you're still here."

THIRTEEN

"Maybe I don't want you to be alone." I shrugged.

"Is that an answer or a question?" He stood up and walked around the side of the table.

When he sat down next to me on the small stone bench, my heart lurched. Being close to him was definitely a problem.

"Maybe we should just let it be what it is." I looked straight down at the remaining food on my plate. I counted the grains of rice, instead of thinking about how his hand rested in the small space between us on the bench, how his smallest finger nearly brushed against my pants. Why had I ever touched his lips? Maybe if I hadn't, none of this would have gotten so complicated. I eased my way a little further away from him.

"Okay, then what is it?" He shifted a little closer to me and spoke in a lower tone. "I'm not the only one feeling it, am I?"

"I don't know." I sighed as my thigh hit the edge of the stone bench and I realized that I had nowhere left to run. "It's nothing." I dared to look in his direction. "It's you, homesick and heartbroken thanks to whoever this Shauna is. It's me, bored and enchanted by something just a little different. It's nothing."

"Nothing." He repeated the word as he looked straight into my eyes. "It doesn't feel like nothing."

"That's all it is." I stood up from the bench.

He caught my hand before I could step away and looked up at me. "Then why are you running?"

"I'm not. I'm just done." I gestured to my empty plate. "Lunch is over, it's time for my next class."

"Maby, I'm sorry, you know." He stood up from the bench as well and made no effort to create space between us. With a subtle tug of his hand he pulled me closer.

"For what?" I caught my breath as I came so close to him that I could detect the faint stubble that sprouted from the curve of his cheek.

"For whatever—whoever—hurt you." He murmured his words as he reached for my other hand. "For whatever happened to keep you trapped so deep inside yourself."

From the tips of my toes to the curve of my lips, my body tingled. His words, coupled with his touch and the intensity of our closeness, sent my mind swirling through fantasies—fantasies that I'd built up over the years in an attempt to avoid the real thing.

"Stop," I whispered as I pulled away from him. What started out as a harmless little game, just a dip of my toe into the possibility of having a crush, had turned into something that crushed my heart in an iron grip. I felt as if I wouldn't breathe again unless his arms were around me.

"Maby, it's okay." He cupped my cheek as I started to turn away. "Just listen to me."

"No. That's the problem." I pushed his hand away and created plenty of distance between us. "I've been listening too much. Listening to your accent, your pretty words, and your arrogance. Listening to all the things that you say to convince other people that you're on top of the world and listening to the truth—that underneath it all, you're terrified of being alone."

"I'm not." He cleared his throat, then looked sharply away. "Fine. I'll drop it. It's not as if this is what I want either." He turned and stalked off across the courtyard.

I stared after him, dazed by both the way I felt about him and the fear that it inspired within me. My plan was to get to college without dating, without falling in love. But Oliver? He threatened all of that. Was it possible that he was just as scared as I was?

Throughout the remainder of my classes, I did my best to think of anything but him. But I wasn't very successful. In fact, by the time I headed back toward the dormitories, my mind was bogged down with thoughts of him. I couldn't be played. He had no intention of staying at Oak Brook. He was just looking for a way to entertain himself and pass the time until he figured out how to get back to England. I wasn't going to be his distraction.

When a reminder popped up on my phone, I smiled to myself. Yes, my riding class would be a perfect distraction. A little time with Aaron—someone I actually had a crush on—would get my focus off Oliver and all his drama. After I dropped off my books and changed into casual clothes, I headed across the courtyard.

I spotted Oliver as I neared the front gate of the campus.

He spotted me too. I felt his eyes lock to mine. His gaze lingered for a long moment, then he looked away and walked over to a group of kids gathered in the courtyard.

Relieved that I wouldn't have to face him, I continued out through the gate. As I hailed a taxi, I recalled the last time Oliver and I visited the city together. My fingertips tingled with the memory of gliding through his hair. My cheeks warmed at the thought of touching his lips.

"Nope, not for long, pal." I settled into the back of the taxi and looked straight ahead. "Aaron is going to erase you from my mind."

At first, it worked. Aaron rode up to me in a sleeveless t-shirt with his hair loose and flowing in the breeze. His skin bronzed by the sunlight and his muscles on full display, he jumped down from the horse to greet me.

It was safe to have a crush on Aaron. He was unattainable. I could enjoy my fantasies and not worry about the drama that might go along with a real boyfriend. But as he greeted me, all I could think of was Oliver scooting closer to me on the bench, his finger grazing against my pants., All I could think of was the way he looked at me when he said my name.

"Mabel, are you listening to me?"

"Sure I am, Ollie." I flashed him a smile as I mounted the horse.

"Aaron." He hung onto the reins until I was settled. Then he squinted up into the sunlight at me.

"Huh?"

"You called me Ollie."

"I most certainly did not." My heart skipped a beat.

"Okay." He shook his head. "I want you to ride solo today, okay? I think it will be good for you and Goldie."

"Okay." I frowned. This was not what I had in mind. How could he distract me from Oliver if he wasn't with me? "Thanks."

I watched as he walked away. Yes, he was still very attractive, but something was different now. I just couldn't get excited to see him. Had I really called him Ollie?

As if the thought of Oliver had summoned him, he stepped out of a taxi that had just pulled up into the driveway. He looked straight at me for a second, then turned his attention to Aaron.

I braced myself for the fireworks I expected to see. What was Oliver doing? I watched him hold his hand out to Aaron. Aaron reluctantly shook it. Oliver offered his most charming smile.

I couldn't hear their conversation, but I did see Aaron nod, then walk him toward the stables. Was he going to let Oliver ride after all? My mind spun as I wondered if Oliver had really come all this way just to be close to me. Was it crazy for me to suspect that? Was it crazy for me not to?

"Unbelievable." I rolled my eyes as I steered the horse onto the trail.

Whatever Oliver was up to, I didn't want to be around to find out.

FOURTEEN

Not long after I'd started down the path, I urged the horse into a gallop. I wanted to get as far away from the stable as I could. Even if Oliver did win over the right to ride a horse, I didn't want him to be able to catch up to me. I needed time to sort out what I was feeling.

As I rode down the familiar path, I recalled the infectious laughter that would often ride along with me. Jennifer's laugh could always bring a smile to my face. She always found a way to be happy. It didn't matter if she'd failed a test or missed a visit yet again with her parents. She always found a way to be cheerful.

I winced as I remembered one particular afternoon that we'd ridden together.

"I think he's adorable. In a bad boy kind of way."

"You're nuts." The memory echoed through my mind. "Stay away from him, Jenny. He's only going to hurt you."

"You're so negative, Maby!" Jennifer had huffed. "Just think about what it will be like kissing him! Those lips!" She smacked her lips and laughed that infectious laugh.

I closed my eyes as I savored the memory of the sound.

Maybe if I hadn't laughed with her. Maybe if I'd been more protective, if I'd insisted that she listen to me, if I had just pinned her down beneath my thumb and kept her there, I wouldn't be alone on our favorite trail.

A crack of thunder caused my eyes to fly open. My heart pounded in reaction to the lightning that followed. I hadn't bothered to check the weather forecast. Usually, Aaron did that. I tightened my grasp on the reins and realized I'd gotten a lot farther from the stable than I thought.

"Alright, it's okay." I did my best to soothe the horse, which began to prance nervously from one side of the trail to the other. Aaron never let me take Goldie out in bad weather—she was very sensitive to it—but this time he had. "Let's go back, we can probably beat the storm—okay, girl?" I tried to guide her into turning around.

Another crack of thunder caused her to bolt forward down the trail instead. I gulped as I gripped the reins and leaned forward against her mane. She moved so fast that I couldn't keep track of where we were headed.

As rain pelted down, my vision became even more blurred. Lightning erupted across the sky in jagged shards. Thick dark clouds nearly blotted out the sun, making it impossible for me to even see if we were still on the trail. The branches and bushes that struck my arms and legs made me suspect that we weren't.

I clung to the reins as tight as I could. With the horse so afraid, there was a good chance she would throw me.

The storm didn't show any signs of letting up as Goldie continued to flee.

When I heard a shout from behind me, I felt some relief. It had to be Aaron.

"Aaron!" I lifted my head enough to call to him. "I'm over here! Aaron! She won't slow down!"

Through the sheets of rain and swirl of movement, I caught

sight of someone who was definitely not Aaron. "Ollie?" The name slipped between my lips as he rode Clover closer to me.

"It's alright, Maby. Just keep holding on. I'll get her to slow down." As he rode up past me, he reached for the reins that I held tight in my hands.

"What are you doing here?" I gulped as another crash of thunder caused the horse to buck into the air beneath me.

"Give me the reins, Maby." He locked his eyes to mine.

"I can't." I frowned. "I'll fall off! She's going too fast!"

"I won't let you fall." He reached for the reins again. "Just let me have them. I can slow her down. You have to trust me."

"Trust you?" My hands trembled at the thought of releasing the reins. How could I, when I had no idea whether he could do what he claimed? But what other choice did I have? If the horse didn't stop soon, she would likely collapse from exhaustion.

"Just try, Maby." He kept Clover right beside me, matching my horse's pace.

As I let go of the reins, I felt him grab onto them. He wrapped them tight around his hand and gave a sharp shout along with a solid yank.

My horse began to slow, just a little at first, then after a few more firm yanks, she settled down into a walk.

With the storm still raging around us, Oliver slid down off Clover and guided Goldie underneath a canopy of tree branches. Then he held his hand up to me.

"Come down, it's not safe for you to be up there."

Wordlessly, I took his hand. As I stared down into his eyes, I tried to make sense of what had just happened.

Oliver had come to my rescue? What might have happened if he hadn't been there?

I landed on the ground beside him, my hand still wrapped up in his.

"Are you hurt?" He squinted through the rain.

"No." I pulled my hand free as my heart raced. "I didn't know it was supposed to storm."

"I don't think anyone did." He glanced back over his shoulder, then looked back at me. "Sorry I wasn't who you were expecting."

"I just assumed Aaron would be out looking for me." I wiped my hair back from my face. The rain just plastered it back down. "Did you steal a horse again?"

"He let me ride it." He shifted closer to me as the wind blew the branches of the trees down toward us.

"Seriously? How did you convince him to do that?"

"I've been told I can be quite charming." He leaned closer as the rain began to subside. "And now I'm a hero, right?"

"Yes." I ducked my head beneath a branch as I met his eyes. "I can't deny that."

"Do you want to?" He ducked beneath the same branch, leaving us mere inches apart.

"I'm glad you showed up when you did." I bit into my bottom lip as I recalled just how scared I was as the horse raced through the woods.

"I started down the trail, then I heard the thunder." He brushed my soaked hair back from my cheek. "I know some horses can't handle storms."

"How do you know?"

"I used to ride a lot. It was one of our favorite things to do." His voice softened as another roll of thunder carried through.

"Yours and Shauna's?" As the rain continued to fall between us, I felt as if we were in a different universe altogether, that Oak Brook Academy wasn't waiting for us, that Aaron wasn't out looking for us both.

"I don't know why I said that." He frowned.

"It's okay to talk about her." I met his eyes.

"I'd rather not."

"Maybe you need to." I placed my hand lightly against his rain-soaked shirt. "Just because you don't want to feel it, doesn't mean you can avoid feeling it."

"I can't feel it." He looked into my eyes. "I can't." He pressed his hand against mine. "It hurts too much. That's why I've tried to stay away from you. I've tried not to be drawn to you. But no matter how hard I try, I can't resist." He shook his head and squeezed my hand. "None of it makes sense. I know that. I know it would be better if I left you alone. But I just can't, Maby."

"I can't either." I had just gotten the words out when Aaron rode up to us.

"Are you both okay?" He frowned as he stared down at us.

I pulled my hand away from Oliver and took a step back. "We're okay. Goldie was just spooked by the storm."

FIFTEEN

"I'm so sorry about that." Aaron shook his head. "I had no idea this storm was coming in. I never would have sent you out on your own—or at all—if I'd known."

"It's alright. I know that." I ran my hands back through my wet hair. "I think it's passed enough now. She'll probably be okay to ride home."

"I'll stay with you to make sure you get back." He looked past me at Oliver. "Thanks for finding her. I'm not sure where you learned to ride, but you definitely have some skills. You might want to think about getting involved in our competitive riding."

"No thanks." Oliver crossed his arms as he stared at Aaron. "I'm not going to be around long enough to compete."

His words struck me hard as he mounted Clover.

That's right, Maby, he's got one foot out the door. You need to stop letting your imagination run wild.

"Sorry to hear that." Aaron offered me his hand to help me up onto Goldie. "Are you sure you feel okay riding her back? She might still be a little nervous."

"I think I'll be okay." I climbed back up onto the horse without looking in Oliver's direction.

"Don't worry, I'll be by your side." Aaron smiled at me.

I waited for the warmth to billow through my stomach in reaction to his kindness and attention. Instead, all I could think about was Oliver's eyes on me.

As I took Goldie's reins, I did my best to focus on the trail ahead. Though the rain had faded to a drizzle, the ground had become muddy and Goldie needed my focus on her.

Aaron remained beside me, just as he'd promised, while Oliver and Clover trotted a short distance behind us. Once the horses were settled in the stable, I pulled out my phone and called for a taxi.

Oliver leaned against the fence of the corral and stared up at the still cloudy sky.

As I walked over to him, I was reminded of his touch on my cheek and the strange way we'd ended up in our own universe.

"Ollie."

"Don't call me that." He frowned.

"Why not?"

"Does it matter?" He looked away from the sky and met my eyes. "I just don't want you to call me it."

"Is it what Shauna calls you?"

"No. No one calls me Ollie." He peered at me with a faint smile on his lips. "No one until you."

"Then I should be allowed to call you it." I shrugged. "It's tradition in my group of friends. Everyone gets a nickname."

"That's why you're Maby?"

"Yes, and now you're Ollie." I leaned back against the fence beside him.

"Does that make me your friend?" He stretched his arms out along the fence.

I became aware of his arm behind my shoulder blades. I did my best not to actually brush up against him.

"Yes, you're my friend." I turned to face him. "You saved me today."

"I was joking about the hero thing." He smiled.

"I wasn't. I could have really been hurt. If you hadn't shown up when you did, I think she might have thrown me. Thank you." I looked into his eyes. "I don't think I said that."

"You're welcome." He tipped his head toward mine. "But I'm still not a hero."

"Maybe not, but you're pretty close."

A horn beeped, alerting me to the presence of the taxi.

"Are you going to ride back with me?"

"Sure. I guess I need to get out of these wet clothes." He tugged at the hem of his shirt, then pulled it up over his head.

I should have looked away, but I just couldn't. The moisture that lingered on his chest glistened in the sunlight that began to peek through the clouds. A second beep from the taxi made me jump.

"You okay?" Oliver looked me over.

"Sure. Yes, fine." I turned and walked toward the taxi. Yet again, I found myself distracted by something that I felt I shouldn't even notice. So what if he was shirtless? So what if he'd rescued me from a wild horse in the middle of a storm? None of that changed the fact that he was going to leave and that I had a rule about not dating while in high school.

He caught up to me at the taxi just as I slid to the far side of the seat. He settled in beside me, then leaned back and closed his eyes.

I stole a look in his direction. His face relaxed when he had his eyes closed. No charming smile, no sharp retort, just a placid expression rippling with subtle sadness. I wanted to know more about him, even though I knew it would do me no good. In that moment, it seemed as if he might be willing to talk.

"She really hurt you, huh?" The question hung heavy in the air between us. I swallowed hard as I realized that it wasn't as casual as it sounded in my head.

"I'm resting. I'm all hero-ed out." He ran his fingertips along the slope of his chest, then placed his hand on the taut muscles of his stomach.

"It's okay, you know. You can talk to me about it. Most of my friends talk to me about what they're dealing with." I shifted in the seat so that I could turn to face him. "It helps and I've been told I'm great at giving advice."

"Great at giving advice about romance when you've never experienced it for yourself?" He opened his eyes just enough to see me. "That doesn't make any sense."

"Maybe it does. Because I've never experienced it, I can have a pure perspective. I'm not blinded by the illusion."

"Love isn't an illusion." He opened his eyes fully and sat forward on the seat. "If you'd ever let yourself feel it, you'd know that."

"You have no idea what you're talking about." I rolled my eyes and looked out the window beside me. "You're not old enough to know what real love is."

"Is that what you really think?" I felt his bare shoulder touch mine as he slid closer to me. "That you have to be a certain age to know what it is?"

"Yes." I refused to look at him as I felt my muscles tighten. Too close—he was far too close.

"Shauna and I dated for four years. We've known each other since we were kids." He lowered his voice. "She was there for me when my grandfather suffered and when he passed away. I was there for her when she lost her little sister. So, was none of that real because we weren't old enough?"

"It sounds like you two have a lot of history." I frowned as I continued to look through the window. "No wonder it hurt so much when things ended."

"Maby." He placed his hand lightly on my knee.

I bit into my bottom lip and refused to look in his direction.

"Pretending we're not old enough to feel things doesn't make it hurt any less. Does it?"

"I wouldn't know. Like you said, I don't have any experience with romance." I felt some relief as I saw Oak Brook come into view.

"Maybe not with romance, but I know you've lost someone."

His words struck me hard. How did he know that? I glanced over at him and instantly I lost myself in his determined eyes. He wanted to know me the same way I wanted to know him.

The taxi pulled to a stop. It took me several seconds to remember that I needed to pay the fare. Once I did and stepped out, I thought I'd be able to make my escape. But he stepped right between me and the gate of the school.

"Tell me, who was it?"

"I don't want to talk about it." I tried to walk around him.

"Maby." He caught me by the shoulder, his hand warm and gentle against me, but his tone stern. "I told you something about me, can't you tell me something about you?"

"You won't understand." I looked into his eyes.

"Try me." He stared back at me.

"I lost my best friend." I stared hard at the sidewalk beneath my shoes. "We didn't have a four-year romance—she didn't die —there's no great tragedy here. I just lost her."

SIXTEEN

"I'm sorry." He gave my shoulder a comforting squeeze. "That must have been hard for you."

"I know, you probably think it's silly. Immature." I peered into his eyes. "But ever since I lost her, it's been hard for me to get close to people. She was more than a friend to me, she was my sister. One minute she was there and the next she was gone."

"Did you two have some kind of fight?" He frowned. "Can't you find a way to work it out?"

"Is that what you're doing with Shauna? Why you keep calling her?" I searched his eyes. "Because you're trying to work it out?"

"Some things are just too broken." His hand fell away from my shoulder. "But yes. For the past few months, I've been thinking that I'd do anything to get her back."

"And now?" I watched his expression closely.

"Now..." He smiled some. "Now, I've found myself forgetting all about her."

"Maybe you're starting to heal." I smiled.

"Maybe I'm ready to move on." He gazed steadily into my eyes.

The intensity of his stare made me take a sharp breath. Did he mean what I thought he meant? Had Oliver really set his sights on me?

"I should get back. You need to get some clothes on." I laughed as I waved to him and hurried through the gate. I could pretend as well as anybody else. I could ignore the undercurrent of attraction between us. I could deny that I wanted to throw myself into his arms and promise him that I could help him get over Shauna.

My mind spun as I made my way back to my dorm room. My heart raced. As confusion filled my thoughts, there was one thing I was certain of. I wanted to be back in the rain with him, with his head tilted so close to mine. I wanted to run my hands across his chest and whisper promises that I would never hurt him the way that Shauna had.

"Unbelievable!" I slammed my bedroom door shut, then threw myself down on my bed. "This can't be happening." I groaned as a mixture of elation and horror flooded through me.

I'd promised myself I'd never go through this, not while I was still in high school, not when I had my future to think about. Yet, there I was, curled up in a ball in my bed, aching for a boy who would never feel the same way about me.

Oliver needed something to take his mind off his pain and I was that something. He could fixate on me and forget about Shauna. He could mend his broken heart by tearing into mine.

I couldn't let that happen. But was it already too late?

A knock on my door jolted me from the chaos that swirled through me. For an instant I thought it might be Oliver, then I heard Fifi's voice.

"Are you in there?" She knocked again. "Maby, what's going

on? Candy said she saw you run in here like someone was chasing you. Are you okay?"

"I'm okay." I sighed as I rested my head against my pillow and closed my eyes.

"You're lying." She opened the door.

"Go away, Fi." I groaned and hid my head under my pillow.

"Everyone is talking about some kind of crazy thing that happened at the stables." She sat down on the edge of my bed. "Were you there?" She plucked the sleeve of my soaked shirt. "I can see you were caught in the rain."

"I was there." I turned over and looked up at her. For a split second I thought she was Jennifer. Then her features came into view. "A storm kicked up and it made my horse go a little crazy."

"Did Aaron save you?" Fifi grinned. "I wouldn't mind being saved by him."

"No, it wasn't Aaron." I pulled my knees up to my chest and wondered if I could tell her the truth. Maybe if I talked about it, I could get it out of my system.

"But someone did save you?" Fifi looked into my eyes. "Alright, you have to spill. I need to know what's going on with you."

"It was Ollie." I winced as I realized I'd used his nickname. "I mean, Oliver. He was the one that saved me."

"Oliver?" Fifi's eyes widened. "I've noticed something going on between the two of you. Is it getting serious?"

"You noticed something?" I scooted closer to her. "What do you mean?"

"He's always looking at you. He'll make a joke and then he looks over at you to see if you laugh. When he walks into a room, he looks at everyone there until he sees you, then he just stops." She shook her head. "I was feeling sorry for him actually, knowing that you won't give him the time of day—you know—because of your rule."

"Of course—because of my rule." I closed my eyes and rested my chin on my knees.

"Unless you're changing that?" Fifi nudged my ankle with her hand. "Maby? Are you going to tell me what's on your mind?"

"The problem is, I can't figure it out." I opened my eyes again and sighed. "I have my rule for a reason, and even if I was to break it, Ollie is not the right person to break it for. He can't wait to get back to England. He broke up with someone he thought he was in love with and he doesn't even know what he wants."

"You mean, you're thinking about it?" She smiled. "Oh wow, I've been waiting for this moment."

"This moment when I screw everything up?" I frowned.

"This moment when your heart opens up." She took my hand and squeezed it. "Falling in love—it's not easy. It never is. But you can't fight it. It only makes it harder."

"I'm not falling in love." I clenched my jaw.

"Okay, sure, you're probably not. So, it should be easy enough for you to walk away from Oliver and not look back. Right?" She looked into my eyes.

"Yes, easy enough." I forced a smile. "Thanks for the talk, Fi, but I think I'm going to take a nap. All the craziness at the stables wore me out."

"Alright. But if you want to talk more, you know where I am." She gave my hand a light pat. As she reached the door, she paused and looked back at me. "I know I'm not Jennifer, and I know it's hard for you to open up to anyone else, but I'll always have your back, you know—for anything you need."

"Thanks, Fi." I managed a small smile, but her words bounced right off me. Everyone said that. Everyone claimed they would always be my friend. But that wasn't how the world worked. I let myself get too close to Jennifer and then she disappeared. I couldn't go through that kind of pain again.

As my chest tightened at the thought, I realized it was a sensation similar to what I felt when I thought about not seeing Oliver again. I squeezed my eyes shut as I realized I had already let things go too far with Oliver. Was it even possible to turn back now?

As my heart raced, I allowed myself—just for a second—to imagine what it would be like to give in. What if I just let it happen? What if I broke my rule? What if I risked getting hurt again?

I imagined his arms around me, his lips nearing mine. I imagined the look in his eyes, the way he would smile at me. I imagined my fingertips gliding through his hair. Warmth that I'd never experienced before spread through my chest, easing the tension there. It spread throughout my body, until I felt as if I could float right up off the bed.

Oliver said that I couldn't understand love because I'd never felt it. Had that changed?

SEVENTEEN

That evening, I decided to skip dinner. I needed time away from Oliver, away from the confusion he created in me. I needed time to think. But no matter how much quiet I had, no matter what pro and con lists I made in my mind, it all came back to chaos.

Underneath it all, I had to admit to one thing, I wanted Oliver. I wanted him more than I'd ever wanted Aaron or any other boy I'd known. I wanted to be close to him, to know everything I could about him, and I certainly wanted to kiss him.

By the time Fifi returned to the room after dinner, I'd gone through every ounce of mental energy I had. Sprawled out on the sofa, I watched as she walked over to me.

"Hey, not hungry?" She crouched down in front of me.

"No, not tonight." I rubbed a hand across my eyes.

"Oliver asked about you at dinner." She frowned. "He was worried about you. Are you sure you didn't get hurt today?"

"No, I'm fine." I sat up and sighed. "I'm just a little lost, I guess."

"A little scared?" Fi sat down beside me. "Maybe?"

"Maybe." I tugged at the hem of my t-shirt. "I just want to hide."

"Running away won't solve anything." She nudged my shoulder with her own. "I'm sure you've given me that advice before."

"It's easier to give than take." I wiped my hands across my face and took a deep breath. "I don't know how I ended up in this mess."

"Maybe it's not a mess." She leaned close to me and lowered her voice. "He's waiting for you in the courtyard."

"What do you mean?" I met her eyes.

"He was worried about you. He asked me to check on you and said that if you wanted to see him, he'd be in the courtyard." She raised an eyebrow. "Maybe you should go sort things out?"

"I'm not sure if there is a way to do that."

"I'm sure there isn't a way to do that from here." She stood up and grabbed my hand. "Let's go. No hiding out."

"I can hide out if I want to." I drew my hand back and glared at her.

"Sure, you can hide out if you want to. But you don't want to, do you?" She put her hands on her hips as she looked at me. "The Maby I know would never let anyone or anything drive her into hiding."

"Ugh, you're so right." I stood up and placed my hands on my hips as well. "This needs to end. One way or the other, it has to stop."

"Good luck." Fi gave me a tight hug. "Just listen to your heart, Maby, and you can't go wrong."

I bit my tongue as I hugged her back. I knew that she meant well, but her words sounded ridiculous to me. Of course I could go wrong by listening to my heart, because somehow my heart had lost its mind. I needed to fix that. If it took seeing Oliver—confronting him face to face—then that was what I would do.

Still in a t-shirt and sweat pants, I marched down the stairs to the common room. Through the windows, I could see him perched on one of the stone benches. He tipped his head back and looked up at the sky.

My heart pounded. Just the sight of him roused something in me that I never expected nor wanted to discover. I pushed open the door and stepped outside.

"Maby." He looked away from the sky and met my eyes.

"I'm fine." I crossed my arms. "You can go now."

"Okay?" He stood up and walked toward me. "You missed dinner."

"I wasn't hungry."

"I don't buy that. I've seen you eat cheesy nachos." He crossed his arms as well as he stared at me.

"What does it matter? I just didn't want to go to dinner tonight."

"Is it because of earlier?" He shoved his hands in his pockets and frowned. "Because of getting caught in the rain with me?"

"Why would it be?" I shook my head as I glanced away.

"You know we both feel it, Maby." He caught my hand just by the fingertips and held it loosely. "But I don't want to be the reason that you don't come to dinner. I don't want you to think that you can't be around me."

"I just needed a breather." I closed my eyes as the warmth from his touch seeped into my skin.

"To get control?" He wrapped his hand tighter around mine. "This isn't something you can pin under your thumb, Maby, it's much more wild than that."

"Wild?" I couldn't help but smile as I felt a jolt of electricity carry through me.

"It's the right way to describe it, isn't it?" He leaned close, his eyes still seeking mine. "Unpredictable, uncontrollable."

"You're not making this any easier on me, Ollie." I pressed my hand against his chest and gave him a solid push back.

"I have no intention of making it easy."

His eyes remained locked to mine, his hand still wrapped around mine. He caught my other hand before I could pull it away from his chest and pressed it there.

"Why not?" I stared at him. "After what happened with Shauna, how could you want this?"

"You're not Shauna." He swallowed hard as he squeezed the hand he held against his chest. "I'm not the same person I was when I was with her either. This is a new time, a new experience. I tried to fight it too, Maby. I really did. I had no intention of coming here and stumbling into you, but here we are."

"Here we are." I frowned as I studied him. "What are we going to do about it?"

"I'm going to start by taking you to dinner." He smiled. "Because I know that you're starving."

"I don't think that's such a good idea." I met his eyes. "Maybe it would be better if we agreed to just stay away from each other."

"That seems pretty impossible, considering that we're literally living in the same place." He tipped his head to the side. "Maybe the better solution is to spend so much time together that we get sick of each other. That might work, right?"

"Maybe." I frowned.

"So dinner?" He offered me his arm.

"We don't have permission to leave campus." I hesitated.

"I got permission." He raised his eyebrows. "Any other excuses?"

"I guess not." I reluctantly wrapped my arm around his. "I am pretty hungry."

"As you should be. We had quite an adventurous day. Look at me, rescuing you again." He patted my arm as he led me toward the gate of the school. "I think I'm getting pretty good at this hero thing."

I cringed. Maybe he was right. Maybe being around him

and his inflated ego would help take care of the ridiculous crush I'd formed. If I spent more time with him, I was sure to see that he wasn't the right person for me.

We walked the short distance to a small restaurant.

As we reached the door, I pulled back some. My mind flashed back to the meals Jennifer and I had shared there. I could hear her laughter as we fought over the last slice of pizza.

"If you don't like Italian, I'm sure we can walk a block and find something else." He met my eyes.

"No, this is fine." I cleared my throat as I stepped inside.

EIGHTEEN

Greasy pizza and wings filled the table within a few minutes of our arrival. I found myself smiling more than I'd expected.

"How do they taste?" Oliver picked up a wing and sniffed it. "Smells hot."

"Tastes hot." I grinned as I took another bite.

"I'm trusting you." He eyed me as he took a bite. "I haven't gotten used to the food around here yet. But this is pretty good."

"Delicious." I sighed as I took another bite. He wasn't wrong; I was starving. But the gnawing feeling in my stomach was far more than that. I'd felt it before—when I was ignoring something I knew to be true.

As he reached across the table and took my hand, I felt the world around us vanish, just like it had when we'd stood together in the rain.

"I want you to take me to your favorite place again—just us this time."

"It's not my favorite place anymore." Though I was tempted, I didn't pull my hand away. I wanted to feel what it was like to just let him hold it.

Immediately, warmth spread through me.

"Why not?" He searched my eyes. "What happened there that changed that?"

"A good friend of mine told me a secret and not long after that she disappeared." I shrugged. "It's a great place to tell secrets."

"Yes, I'm sure it is. I'm sorry you lost your friend." He squeezed my hand. "Do you want to tell me what happened?"

"No, I want to show you my new favorite place." I pulled my hand free of his and stood up from the table.

"Okay, that sounds good to me." He stood up as well and left some cash on the table. "Should I get us a taxi?"

"No need. My favorite place is back at Oak Brook." I smiled as I led him out the door.

When he took my hand again, a surge of happiness rushed through me. Maybe this wasn't so bad. Maybe it could be wonderful if I just let it be.

"Please tell me it's not going to be a classroom." He laughed as he followed after me. "Your favorite place is not allowed to be school."

"And why not?" I glanced over my shoulder at him and grinned. "Don't worry, it's not a classroom."

"Then what is it?" He fell into step beside me.

"It's a secret place, a sacred place." I ushered him through the gate and noticed a flicker of light as a guard shined his flashlight in our direction.

"Hurry." Oliver steered me away from the light.

"You didn't get permission, did you?" I frowned as I dodged the attention of the guard.

"Not technically, no." He cringed as he broke into a run and tugged me along behind him.

"Not at all, you mean?" I pushed him between two buildings, into the darkness that the alley provided.

"I just wanted us to have a good night." He met my eyes.

I gave him another firm push until his back was against the wall of the alley. As I stared at him and my heart pumped with a mixture of excitement and fear, I wanted to be angry. I wanted to tell him how irresponsible and reckless he was.

Instead, my hands lingered on his chest and kept him pinned against the wall.

"Are you having a good night?"

"The best." He murmured his words and started to push up against my hands as he reached for me.

"Stay." I pushed him back again, then draped my body over his. As my cheek brushed against his, I ducked my head into the curve of his neck just in time to avoid the beam of the flashlight that shone down the alley. "Be still," I whispered to him as his arms wrapped around me.

All at once, I was enveloped by him, something that I'd fantasized about. It felt so much better than I could have ever imagined. My entire body tingled as warmth spread to the very tips of my toes. I heard the guard walk away.

I knew the danger had passed, but I didn't pull away and neither did he. Instead, his arms tightened around me. His lips lightly touched the strands of my hair that covered my ear as he spoke to me.

"Don't ask me to let you go, Maby. Please."

The warmth of his breath coasted across my sensitive skin as his body remained curled around mine. He spoke so softly that I almost thought I'd imagined his words.

When he pulled away, I thought maybe I had, because he looked down the alley instead of at me.

"I think he's gone."

I stared at him, stunned and uncertain what to think of what he'd said to me.

"Ollie."

"I know, I'm sorry." He turned back to face me, though

leaving some distance between us. "I screwed up again. I never should have lied to you."

"It's not that." I touched his cheek. "I mean, I'd rather you didn't lie to me. But I still want to show you my favorite place. Do you want to see it?"

"Yes." He took my hand. "Absolutely."

"This way." I led him down the alley to the next section of buildings and past them until we reached another part of the campus that was rarely used. The buildings in this section had been slated for storage, and one in particular had been claimed by me.

As we neared it, I turned to face him. "If I show you this, you have to promise to keep it a secret."

"I promise." He stared at me intently.

"I mean it. It's not just my place. It's a place for all my friends to go—to get away from everything. You're one of us now, Ollie, but I need to trust that you're going to keep our secret." I looked into his eyes. "Can I trust you?"

"Yes." He breathed the word as he stepped closer to me. "Always, Maby. I will keep your secret and I'm glad to be considered your friend."

Friend, I reminded myself. Friend—just keep it like that. Don't think about his arms around you, don't think about his lips against your hair. Just focus on the friendship.

"Okay, let's go inside." I smiled as I turned the knob on the door.

Opening the door to the hideout never got old to me. It always felt like coming home. Between the cushions piled up in the middle of the floor, the curtains hung up in strange places, and Apple's artwork on the walls, I felt surrounded by the people I loved and trusted the most.

"I know it probably doesn't look like much."

"It looks like you." He pulled the door closed behind us.

"Like me?" I laughed as I turned to face him.

"Full of love." He slid his arms around my waist and looked into my eyes. "Welcoming and warm."

"Is that what you think?" I felt that surge of warmth again and this time the tingling spread to my lips.

"It's what I know." He tipped his head toward mine. "I know I haven't made the best impression since I arrived. I know I gave you a bit of a hard time. I'm sorry for that. You scared me."

"I scared you?" I raised an eyebrow. "How?"

"When things ended with Shauna, I thought I'd never be okay again. But the first moment I saw you, I felt this spark." He frowned, then shook his head. "I didn't think it was possible."

"Is that what you felt when you met Shauna?"

"It was ten thousand times stronger than what I felt when I met Shauna. It was like nothing I'd ever felt before." He rested his forehead against mine and spoke in the same soft whisper he'd used earlier in the evening. "I feel it now."

"So do I." My eyes fell closed as my mind swam with dizziness. I no longer wanted to be careful, I didn't care about my rule about not dating in high school, I didn't care about his not being over Shauna.

All I cared about was how close our lips were, so close that I could almost feel the warmth that emanated from his. All I had to do was lift my chin and tip my head. My heart pounded so hard I thought it might explode.

NINETEEN

The growl of an engine right outside the door broke the magic of the moment just as my lips neared his. I pulled back and looked toward the window. Headlights shone outside the building. I put my finger to my lips as I looked back at Oliver.

He nodded, then remained perfectly still.

The engine idled for a few seconds, then the vehicle turned and drove back the other way.

"They're looking for us." I frowned.

"They're gone now." He wrapped his arms around my waist again—this time from behind me—and touched his lips to the back of my head. "We can relax."

"We should get back." I turned around in his arms to face him. "Sneaking around is one thing, but missing curfew, that's another."

"Those rules again." He sighed as his gaze moved across my face. "Can't we just get back to thirty seconds ago? I think we were in the middle of something."

"I think we were too." I caressed the curve of his cheek. "But maybe it's good that we got interrupted."

"Why? Why is it good?" He cupped my cheeks and looked into my eyes. "I don't think it's good at all."

"Ollie, all of this is wonderful. I can't say that it isn't. But it's also surprising and I feel like I'm trying to catch up."

"Is this your 'it's not you, it's me' speech?" He sighed as he let his hands fall back to his sides.

"No, it's not that." I caught his hands and held them tight. "It's my 'let's take this slow and see where it goes' speech. Let's not rush into anything."

"I'm not sure I can be patient." He frowned as he studied me. "I'm trying. I swear I am. But I've never felt this kind of draw before. I know you're scared. I don't want you to give up before we even have a chance."

"I won't."

"You'll run from it." He pulled me closer. "You'll talk yourself out of it." He dipped his lips close to mine. "Why can't we just let it flow?"

My lips ached as his drifted just past them. I rocked forward on the tips of my toes a moment too late to kiss him.

He took a sharp breath, then sought my lips again, this time with determination.

I pulled back as my mind swirled. "Ollie." I winced. "Please, I need you to be patient with me."

"I will." He pressed his lips against my forehead instead. "If that's what you want, then that's what I'll be." He leaned back and looked into my eyes. "I'll play by your rules, Maby, but the moment you want something different, all you have to do is tell me. Will you tell me?"

"Yes." As he leaned back, I met his eyes. "I promise."

"Good." He brushed his hands back through my hair and sighed as they came to rest on my shoulders. "I never expected this. I fought my father so hard when he insisted I get away for a while. Now all I can think about is how grateful I am that he insisted."

I smiled at his words, but they also reminded me that he wouldn't always be here. He still wanted to go back to England and he'd come here to escape heartbreak. How could anything possibly work between us?

Just let it flow, I reminded myself. *Just see where it takes you.*

As we walked back to the dorms, I felt such a sudden urge to speak to Jennifer. I wanted to tell her about Oliver, my racing heart, and the almost kiss. The urge shifted into pain as I realized that I couldn't.

"Maby, are you okay?" Oliver paused at the bottom of the stairs that led to the girls' dormitory.

"I'm fine." I forced a smile.

"You're not." He frowned as he looked into my eyes. "What's going on?"

"Just missing someone."

"Your friend?" He shook his head. "What happened between you two?"

"It's a long story."

"One I'd like to hear."

"Another time." I smiled again, then glanced at the clock on the wall. "Get back to your dorm before you get into trouble."

"Good night, Maby." He caught my hand and brought it to his lips for a light kiss.

"Good night, Ollie." I headed up the stairs to my dorm room. Still, I wondered what I was getting myself into...

When I opened the door, I heard Fifi's subtle snoring. At least I wouldn't have to give her an explanation. Once I was safely in my own room, I sat down on my bed and closed my eyes. Already I regretted not kissing him. Why hadn't I just gone for it? It was what I wanted, it was what he wanted. What harm could it do?

I closed my eyes as I remembered another night. The night I tried to talk Jenny out of seeing a boy I didn't like.

"What harm could it do?" Jennifer had laughed as she'd sprawled out on the bed beside me.

"He's a player, Jenny, and he's irresponsible." I had sprawled out on the bed beside her. We stared into each other's eyes.

"But when he kissed me, it was like the ocean and the moon—"

"And the birds and the bees? Bees sting, remember?"

We'd stayed up all night that night. We'd argued some, laughed some, even cried some. But in the end, she still wanted to be with him and no warning from me could stop her.

"Maybe I just didn't try hard enough." My chest ached at the thought. "Maybe I just didn't say the right thing."

I picked up my phone and began to look through hundreds of pictures of the two of us. My dislike of her new boyfriend had driven a wedge between us, but it hadn't been enough to keep us apart. I'd promised her that I would help her however I could, but one day she was just gone. Not a word, not a goodbye, not an explanation.

"We were supposed to take on the world together, Jenny." I sighed as I looked at her picture. "Now I have no idea what I'm doing. Now I know what you meant when you talked about him. I know how it feels."

I set my phone down and lost myself in the memory of Oliver's arms around me. Could it really be love that I was feeling? It was certainly more powerful than anything I'd ever experienced before. But was that just because it was new? Because it was different? Because of that dreamy accent that made everything he said sound so enticing?

I remembered how harshly I'd judged Jennifer—my best friend, my sister—when she'd tried to explain how things could go too far, how she could make such a big mistake. I'd been selfish.

I squeezed my eyes shut as tears began to flow. I hadn't listened to what she had to say, I'd just thought about how everything would change.

When I'd pressed my ear against the tiles and she'd whispered her secret to me, it felt like my entire life changed. But it was her life that had been permanently altered, and instead of being the friend she needed, I got angry.

Maybe she wouldn't have disappeared if I'd tried harder, if I'd promised her that everything would be okay. Maybe she wouldn't have changed her number and ignored my emails. Love could be a more powerful thing than I ever knew. She'd gotten caught up in the heat of the moment, she'd made a mistake, but I'd made one too.

As my mind drifted back to Oliver and the intensity of the feelings I had for him, I realized now that I was the one who needed to be careful. I couldn't wait to see him again, but I needed to be careful.

TWENTY

I woke up to a knock on my door early the next morning.

"Maby? Are you up? Wake up!"

"I'm up, I'm up." I groaned as I threw a pillow at the door. "What do you want, Fi?"

"I want details!" She knocked even harder.

I couldn't help but laugh at her enthusiasm. As I pushed myself out of bed, I realized that my smile lingered. It was a rare thing for me to feel so cheerful in the morning. Maybe Oliver being around wasn't such a bad thing.

When I opened the door, Fifi practically tumbled inside.

"I know you went off campus last night." She grinned at me as she settled on the end of the bed. "You have to tell me everything."

"There's not much to tell." I shrugged. "We just went to dinner."

"Liar." She threw a pillow at me. "Oh, you're holding back on me! Why?"

"I just can't." I began to pace through the room. My hands knotted together as I attempted to settle the emotions that raced through me.

"You're not happy?" Fi stood up from the bed and walked over to me. "Did he do something to hurt you?"

"No, not at all." I took a deep breath, then sighed. "This just wasn't part of my plan."

"It never is." Fifi frowned as she studied me. "I know that out of all of us, you're the most determined to make it to college without any distractions, but life doesn't work that way, Maby. Sometimes the right person comes along at the wrong time and you have to decide what's more important, your plans or your heart."

"I just feel like it's all crazy." I turned to face her. "The more I try to control it, the less in control I feel."

"So, don't try to control it. Be honest with yourself. What will you regret more, being with him and seeing where things go or denying your feelings and missing your chance to find out?"

"You don't have to be so logical about it." I frowned. "That's supposed to be my job."

"That's my point, though. Logic isn't even a factor here. You can't count on it to get you through this. You have to really dig deep and figure out what it is that you want." She shrugged. "You don't have to choose Oliver, but you have to be honest with yourself."

"Easier said than done, I think." I blew air from between my lips and placed my hands on my hips. "I'm used to things being pretty simple."

"Unfortunately, there's nothing simple about this." She shook her head. "Make sure you get some breakfast. Being in love on an empty stomach can be very nauseating."

I held my breath as she left my room. Was that what I was experiencing? Being in love? Sure, there was no question that I was attracted to him, that I hadn't been able to stop thinking about him, but did that mean that I was in love?

I went through the motions of getting ready for school and

managed to eat half a bagel. But my mind remained fixated on the idea that I might be in love. I'd always rolled my eyes at my friends when they claimed to have fallen in love, because it seemed impossible at a young age.

My heart raced at the thought of seeing Oliver again, at the memory of his lips seeking mine. A tingle tickled at my lips as I smiled to myself, lost in the fantasy of what it would be like to actually kiss him.

By the time I made it to my first class, my thoughts were torn between fantasy and reality—the fantasy of his arms wrapped around me and the reality of his desire to return to England.

Throughout each class, I found it hard to concentrate. Schoolwork normally came easily to me, at least easily enough to provide the grades that I needed. But with Oliver on my mind, I seemed to be making foolish mistakes.

"Mabel, do you need to go to the nurse?" My math teacher dropped my practice test on my desk and looked into my eyes. "Are you not feeling well?"

I stared down at the red marks all over my paper. How could I have gotten that many problems wrong?

"I'm fine. I'm sorry, I'm just a little distracted today."

"Snap out of it." She gave my shoulder a light pat, then returned to the front of the room.

Snap out of it. The words echoed through my mind as the bell rang for lunch. Maybe that was what I needed to do.

I prepared myself to see Oliver again as I walked toward the cafeteria. Maybe the newness and excitement wouldn't be as strong. Maybe it had worn off. But as I neared the entrance of the cafeteria, I spotted him in the hallway near the door and instantly my mind swirled with a mixture of pleasure and nervousness. I noticed that he had his phone pressed against his ear.

"I've been waiting for your call." He paused, then spoke again, this time a little sharper. "I know about the time difference, but you knew I needed to talk to you. Did you get my texts?"

My heart dropped as I heard the determination in his voice. Clearly he was still trying to make things work with Shauna. He'd said he'd be patient. He'd said that they could let things flow because he likely wanted to keep his options open.

"I hear you, Shauna, I do, but please, you have to think this through. Please, just reconsider it. I know it's all my fault and I'm so sorry. I hope you can forgive me."

He hopes she can forgive him? My stomach twisted into a knot. Yes, Oliver was in love with someone, but it wasn't me. He was still in love with Shauna. Not that I should have expected anything different.

My hands trembled as I clutched the straps of my backpack. I knew that in just a second he would turn to look at me and find me frozen there, with my bottom lip pathetically shaking and my emotions spilled all over the floor.

I couldn't let that happen.

Instead, I turned and hurried down another hall that led out to the courtyard. I couldn't imagine eating a bite of food.

I'd let him get under my skin. I'd let him convince me that he felt something real for me. But the only thing he truly felt was for Shauna. Maybe it was for the best, maybe they were the ones that belonged together. But even if that was true, it didn't make my heart ache any less.

As I ran through the courtyard, I felt dizzy and sick at the same time. How could I have let myself be so vulnerable?

I closed myself off in the hideout and immediately thought about Jennifer. Had she felt this alone? Had it been even worse for her? It broke my heart even more to think that she had suffered this way and I hadn't been there for her when she needed me.

What kind of friend was I?

"I'm so sorry, Jenny." I pulled my knees to my chest and wept into them. I cried not just for Oliver's betrayal, but for my friend who had likely shed just as many if not more tears than me. I cried because I'd lost sight of my plan, of my future, all for the sake of some boy who clearly did not feel the same way about me.

After a few minutes, I wiped my tears. I took a deep breath and stood up. Now that I knew I'd been right from the start in terms of avoiding relationships at all costs, I would have to be strong and do just that.

Let Oliver get back with Shauna, let him go back to England. It would make avoiding him that much easier.

It would take some time, but I could get him out of my system.

TWENTY-ONE

I spent the rest of the day relieved that I didn't share any classes with Oliver. At the end of my last class, I noticed him in the hallway not far away. Despite the sudden rush of excitement I felt to see him, I turned quickly and headed in the other direction.

Soon enough, I was sure, that excitement would wear off. But for now, the best plan of action was to stay as far away from Oliver as possible.

As I headed out into the courtyard, the sky rumbled above me. Another thunderstorm was on its way. The sound reminded me of us getting caught together in the rain. Would it always? My chest tightened and I clenched my jaw. I couldn't let it. I had to stop all of this from happening.

As I walked in the direction of the hideout, the people around me began to scatter to escape the rain. Soon I heard only one set of footsteps. I ignored them at first.

When I turned down the alley that would lead me to the hideout, I realized the footsteps were still behind me. I stopped and glanced back over my shoulder.

Oliver, his hair already slick from the light rain that had started to fall, locked his eyes to mine and stared back at me.

"Are you following me?" The words popped out of my mouth as another roll of thunder crashed above us.

"Are you avoiding me?" He shoved his hands into his pockets as a burst of wind ruffled his loose t-shirt.

"I don't know what you're talking about." I shrugged.

"Why lie about it?" He took a few steps, then paused, still a short distance from me. "You weren't at lunch. You haven't answered my texts. When I saw you in the hallway, you ran away." He narrowed his eyes. "Why would you do that?"

"Why does it matter? We said we were keeping things casual, right?" I licked my lips as I wondered how to say what I had to say. Was I ready to tell him that I was done? That I never wanted to see him again? My eyes misted with tears at the thought.

"Casual doesn't mean avoiding each other like the plague." He crossed the small amount of distance that remained and peered through the lightly falling raindrops at me. "What's going on, Maby?"

"I just think it's best if we spend less time together." My voice wavered with each word that I spoke. I tried to remember how desperate he'd sounded on the phone when he'd spoken to Shauna. I tried to remind myself that it wasn't me that he was after. But the way he looked at me—as if he wanted to see into the depths of me—it made me wonder if I was wrong.

"I knew it." He frowned as he glanced away from me. "I knew you would get scared and talk yourself out of all this. Didn't I say that?" His jaw tensed as he looked back at me. "You don't have to be scared, Maby."

"I'm not scared." I felt a sudden surge of anger. How dare he lie to me? How dare he say that I didn't need to be scared when I knew the truth? "I told you before, this isn't part of my plan. I'm not going to let some silly crush take my entire future away, I'm not going to do it!" I took a step back and held up my hands. "Just get over it, Oliver, okay? Soon enough you'll be back in England and living the life you really want."

"Get over it?" His eyes flashed, despite the clouds that covered any hint of sunlight. He reached for my hand as if he might grab it but stopped at the last second. "How am I ever supposed to get over you, Maby?" He let his hand fall back to his side as he drew a heavy breath. "I guess I'm the idiot here for thinking that you felt even close to the same way about me as I feel about you."

"Enough, Oliver, enough with the dramatics. Okay?" I rolled my eyes. "I'm sure you can find someone else to pass your time with—to keep yourself entertained—until you get what you actually want."

"Why would you say that to me?" He glared at me. When he spoke again, his voice shook. "Is that what you really think of me? That I'm just some kind of manipulative user that's out to hurt you? Where is all this coming from?"

"Never mind, Oliver. Just drop it. It doesn't matter anyway, right? It's not like we even kissed." I bit into my bottom lip as a hint of regret threatened to flood my eyes with tears. Maybe I should have kissed him, just once, just to see what it would be like. "You're the mysterious new guy with the sexy accent. You can have any girl here; just go find someone new to follow."

"Wow." He ran his hands back through his damp hair. "Maybe I didn't know you at all, if this is the way that you can think of me. Fine, if that's what you want, I'll go." He turned and started to walk away.

With each step he took, I felt as if my entire world had begun to collapse. I wanted more than anything to call out to him, but I kept my lips sealed shut. I couldn't survive his choosing Shauna over me. I couldn't trust him, when all he said appeared to be lies.

"No!" He turned back suddenly and strode right over to me. "I won't. I won't just walk away from you." He stared into my eyes as his hands curved around my shoulders. "Maby, just tell me, please. Why? Is that so much to ask of you?"

I continued to keep my mouth locked shut. If I opened it, I had no idea what I might say, what I might do. As rain streaked down his face, I could see the pain dug into the ridges and grooves of his handsome features. Was I really the cause of that?

"Am I just that terrible?" He shivered. "Do I mean so little to you that you can just toss me aside like garbage?"

"Stop." I cupped his cheeks as my urge to soothe him overtook me and forced my lips apart. "Stop lying to me, Oliver."

"I'm not lying." He settled his hands on top of mine and held them against his cheeks. "I don't know why you think I am. Maybe it's because of the friend that you lost, maybe it's because of your rules. But I'll do anything if it means that you'll give me a chance."

I wanted to believe him. I wanted to throw my arms around him and hold him close. I wished I'd never overheard his conversation with Shauna. I could still be living in blissful ignorance and enjoying the affection he offered me instead of being ripped apart by my own emotions and desire.

"It's not right, Oliver. I'm sorry." I let my hands slip out from under his and fall back to my sides. "Please, don't make me say why."

"Just talk to me." He caught my hands and gave them a gentle squeeze. "Just tell me what's going on. What did I do? Is it Aaron? Is that it? It's not right. He's too old for you!"

"Ugh, no." I shook my head and sighed. "Of course it's not Aaron. He would never do that; neither would I."

"So it's someone else then?" He tipped his head toward

mine. "Tell me the truth. You don't want to be with me because there's someone else." His gaze locked to mine, our eyes only inches apart.

"Yes." I whispered the word as I ignored my desire to pull him into my arms, to touch every inch of his skin that I could reach. "It's someone else."

"I can't believe it." He released my hands and turned away from me. "I'm such an idiot. I can't believe I've let this happen to me again."

As he jogged off through the rain and the puddles that had begun to form, I felt as if he'd taken a huge piece of me with him.

TWENTY-TWO

"What was that all about?"

The voice from the alley startled me. I turned to find Candy in the shadows behind me.

"Candy, I didn't know you were there." I pressed my hand against my forehead as I tried to settle my emotions.

"I thought you said you weren't interested?" She raised an eyebrow and crossed her arms. "I've been making a lot of effort to get his attention and the whole time you've had something going with him behind my back?"

"No, it's not like that." I met her eyes. "I didn't expect anything to happen between us, but then it just sort of did."

"Sort of did?" She frowned. "I'm not sure that's even possible."

"You know my rules, Candy. I'm not supposed to date while I'm in high school and I take that very seriously. But there was just something about Oliver, something that drew me in." I took her hand. "Trust me, Candy, there's nothing between us now."

"It didn't look like nothing." She pulled her hand away. "It looked like the two of you belonged on the cover of some kind of teenage romance novel. I mean really? The way he looked at you, the way you grabbed his face." She scrunched up her nose. "That's not nothing."

"You're right." I sighed and closed my eyes. "It's not nothing. At least not yet. But it's going to turn into nothing. I'm going to stay away from him and whatever these weird mixed-up feelings are inside—they are going to disappear. I don't want anything to come between us. You know that, don't you?"

"I don't know what to think." Candy stared hard at the ground. "Maybe you thought I was desperate enough not to notice you playing this little game, but I'm not. Yes, I don't have a boyfriend, but that doesn't mean I'll take yours off your hands." She put her hands on her hips as she looked up at me. "I have feelings, you know, Maby. I really thought he liked me. And you let me think that, all the while knowing he was head-over-heels in love with you."

"No, that's not true." I stepped in front of her as she tried to walk past. "It's not true. He doesn't really feel that way about me. The truth is, he's still hung up on his girlfriend back in England. He doesn't love me, he doesn't have feelings for me, he just wants someone to keep him company until he can get back into Shauna's good graces." I pursed my lips at the thought.

"Seriously? He's still into his ex?" She frowned.

"He is. If you want to just have some fun, I'm sure that he'd be up for it, but if you want anything more than that, I wouldn't touch him with a ten-foot pole. He will con you into thinking he's in love with you, but the truth is, he only wants Shauna."

"Maby, that still doesn't explain why you didn't just tell me the truth. All you had to do was say, hey Candy, I've got a thing for Oliver now."

"I was fighting it. I didn't think it was anything real. I thought seeing him with you would make it easier for me to let go of those weird feelings."

"But it didn't. Because you don't respect me as a friend." She shook her head. "I know you never would have done anything like this to Jenny."

"Candy." I took a sharp breath.

"It's true. Yes, I said it!" She glared at me. "We all know that you and Jenny were the closest out of all of us. When she went away, I thought maybe we'd get closer, but instead you've shut everybody out. Yes, you're there whenever we need you, but you're not really there." She tilted her head to the side as she studied me. "You just pretend to care. I'm sorry I didn't see it sooner."

"Candy! I don't pretend. I do care!" I reached my arms out to her.

"No, don't!" She stepped back. "Just stop. I'm sorry that you lost Jenny, I really am. But you're not the only one who lost her. We all lost her. Then we all lost you too." She shook her head. "We used to be a family."

"We still are. I swear it, Candy!" Panic flooded me as I felt everything that I held dear slip away.

"It's not true, Maby. When Jenny left, you broke inside, and instead of turning to your friends to help you heal, you turned away from all of us. I've tried to be there for you. I've tried to talk to you about Jenny, but you shut me down every time."

"I'm sorry." I stared at her as I realized that she was right. "I'm sorry, I just can't talk about Jenny."

"Because she left you. Because she made a mistake that you couldn't forgive."

"Because I didn't protect her!" I clasped my hands into fists at my sides. "Because when she needed me most, I wasn't there for her. Because maybe if I had tried harder, she wouldn't have disappeared!" My knees grew weak as grief caused all my muscles to clamp down.

"Oh, Maby." Candy sighed as she touched my cheek and

looked into my eyes. "When are you going to get it through your head that you're not in charge of everyone? Jenny did what she did because she wanted to. Because in that moment, all that mattered to her was what she was feeling. It happens. She didn't do it because you weren't a good enough friend." She let her hand fall away as she sighed. "I wish you would have told me the truth about what you were feeling all that time."

"I wish I had too." I looked into her eyes. "And I'm sorry that I didn't tell you the truth about how I felt about Oliver. But it's over now. I swear it."

"I wish I could believe that." She frowned as she pushed past me, back toward the dorm. "I just need some time to figure this all out. Please, just let me have that."

As I watched her walk away, I flashed back to a few minutes before, when Oliver had done the same thing.

Why did I always end up alone? Why did people find it so easy to turn and walk out of my life?

I understood why Candy was upset with me. But that didn't make it hurt any less when she didn't look back over her shoulder. There was only one place I could go to let my feelings out, only one place I felt safe enough to truly let go.

As I ran toward the hideout, I wished with all my heart that I could just have one chance to change things. I would go back to Jenny the night we stayed up all night talking and I would demand that she break things off with her boyfriend or at the very least promise that she would be careful. Maybe if I had tried harder...

I collapsed onto the pile of pillows on the floor and closed my eyes as tears began to flow. I'd already lost Jenny and now I was about to lose Candy too. How many more people would I have to say goodbye to in my life?

I rolled over on the pillows and looked up at the ceiling. Maybe one day I would understand the emotions that threatened to suffocate me, but at the moment all I knew was chaos. Lost in the fog of anger, hurt, and regret, I almost didn't hear the subtle knock at the door. The second knock—stronger—caused me to jump out of my skin. I sat up and stared hard at the door.

Who would be knocking?

TWENTY-THREE

I wiped my face clean as I walked toward the door. If it was one of my friends, I couldn't let them see how upset I was. Candy had been right about that. I had been hiding my true feelings for a long time. As I opened the door, I prepared myself to see anyone on the other side—except for the person I found there.

"Oliver."

"It's Ollie, isn't it?" He looked into my eyes. "Or is that over now too?"

I swallowed hard as I felt a surge of desire for him, followed by anger that I couldn't control it.

"I need space. I need time for this to stop being so intense." I backed away from the door and started to close it.

"Wait." He put his hand on the door to stop it. "I deserve more than that. After what happened with Shauna I promised myself that I wouldn't let anyone treat me like that again."

"I'm not trying to treat you badly." I sighed as I took a step back and allowed him to step inside.

"Then just tell me the truth. That's all I'm asking for. What is it about falling in love that's so horrifying for you? What is the worst that could happen?"

"The worst that could happen?" I stared straight into his eyes. "I could get lost in these feelings for you and make a mistake that changes my entire life. My best friend, someone I thought would always be part of my life, made a mistake and she disappeared from my life because of it."

"What do you mean by a mistake?" He narrowed his eyes. "What happened to your friend? Did she take off with some guy? Did she hurt herself? What happened?" He caught my arms just above the elbows as I tried to turn away. "You can tell me, Maby. You can finally let it out."

"She got pregnant. Okay?" I tried to ignore the powerful feeling that his touch on my arms created within me. "She lost herself in her feelings for some guy who only wanted one thing, and when he asked her not to be careful—just one time—she made a terrible mistake. Next thing I knew, she was gone. Like, vanished. One day she was here, the next she was gone. Her number was changed, all her social media was shut down, she stopped answering my e-mails."

"I'm sorry about that." He tightened his grasp on my arms and looked into my eyes. "But that's not what would happen with us. I promise you that."

"Yes, because I won't let it. Before all this happened, Jenny and I were on the same page. Neither of us were going to date in high school, we had our futures planned out, and we were always going to be there for one another." I bit into my bottom lip as tears threatened my eyes. "I can't go through that again."

"You think I would vanish on you like that?" He ran his thumbs along the sleeves of my blouse and shook his head. "I would never do that to you."

"You are such a liar." I pulled my arms free from his grasp. "I know what you really want, Oliver. I know you want to go back to England. You want to go back to Shauna. Me? I'm just a way to distract yourself while you're here."

"Don't say that!" He frowned as he followed me toward the rear of the building. "It's not true, Maby."

"Stop, just stop lying to me." I turned back to face him. "How stupid do you think I am?" I glared at him. "I'll admit, I let myself get caught up in you. I'm not even sure how it happened. I'm really not. Because I didn't want it to happen."

"Neither did I." He winced. "When I first arrived, I felt a spark with you and it scared me."

"Why?" I stared into his eyes.

"Because." He frowned as he looked at me. "I didn't want to be hurt again. I didn't want to go through heartbreak again. So, I tried to ignore it. I tried to push it away by being a bit of a jerk." He shook his head. "But it didn't work. Every time I saw you, the spark just got stronger. I know it doesn't seem like the right time, Maby. I know that I'm just coming out of a break-up and you have no real reason to trust me. But, just like you, I couldn't fight it. Doesn't that tell you something?" He caressed my cheek as he studied me. "Doesn't it tell us both something?"

"Yes." I licked my lips as his fingertips lingered on my cheek. "It tells us that this is nothing more than hormones and crazy emotions. I'm hurt and lonely because Jenny isn't here and you're heartbroken over a girl who just wasn't that into you. It tells me that we're trying to use each other to drown our sorrows. It tells me that none of what we're feeling is real. It's just an illusion to make us feel better about ourselves."

"You think you know so much." He drew his hand away and tapped his chest with his fist. "I know what I feel, you don't get to tell me what I feel. You don't know anything about what happened between me and Shauna." He scowled at me, then glanced away. "You assume too much."

"Then tell me." I dared to meet his eyes as he looked back at me. "Tell me, what did I get wrong? You're in love with her, aren't you? You want her back, don't you?"

He stared at me, his lips tight, but he didn't say a word. Instead, he walked toward me until I backed up against the wall of the building.

"I was in love with her, yes," he whispered and looked straight into my eyes. "And don't tell me that it's not possible. We'd liked one another since we were twelve. Never once did it cross my mind that there would be a time in my life that Shauna wasn't at my side. She was as much a part of my life as the breath that I took. I trusted her more than I trusted my own family. I thought she felt the same way." He glanced away from me, took a slow breath, then looked back into my eyes. "Until I walked in on her in her bedroom with a friend of mine." His lips quivered as he continued. "She told me she was sick that night, so I wanted to bring her some soup. I wanted to keep her company and watch a movie together. But when I got there, she wasn't sick. She was wrapped up in her sheets with someone we both considered to be a friend."

"Ollie, I'm so sorry." My heart ached for him as I read the pain in his eyes and heard the shudder in his voice. "I can't even imagine how you must have felt."

"No, you can't." He ran his hand back through his hair and sighed. "I'm not proud of how I acted. I was angry, I threw some things, and the next day, I wouldn't stop calling her. I just wanted an explanation. I just wanted to know why she did what she did. I didn't think it was wrong for me to want that."

"It wasn't." I frowned. "You just wanted to understand how you could be erased."

"Exactly." He shook his head. "I should have just let it go, but I couldn't. That's when my dad insisted I take a break and come here, so that I could clear my head and have some distance from her."

"It wasn't a bad idea." I took a deep breath, then crossed my arms as I looked at him. "But it wasn't enough, was it?"

TWENTY-FOUR

"What's that supposed to mean?" He frowned as he searched my eyes.

"Nothing." I glanced away.

"No, tell me." He stepped to the side to meet my eyes again. "Please, Maby, I can't be left in the dark again. With Shauna, all I wanted to know was how she could be with this other guy. I just wanted to know what changed in her, what I did to make her change that allowed her to hurt me like that." He drew a heavy breath. "I know that you don't owe me anything. But I can't walk away without having some kind of explanation. I don't think it's too much to ask."

"You still want her, Ollie." I shivered as his name rolled off my tongue. I wanted to be immune to his touch, to his eyes, to the sound of his name, but I wasn't. My knees were just as weak as they had been when he put his arms around me for the first time—if not a little more.

"No, I don't." He narrowed his eyes. "That's all behind me now."

"Don't lie." I sighed and closed my eyes.

"I'm not lying, Maby." He slid his arms around my waist

and pulled me close to him. "I don't know why you think I am, but I'm not lying. Shauna and I—we're always going to have a history—but that's all it is, history."

"See, this is what proves to me that you can't care about me, not even a little bit." I pulled away from his embrace.

"How can you say that?"

"How can I? Because I know the truth." I fought back a wave of hurt and forced the words from between my lips. "I heard you on the phone. I heard you begging her to give you another chance."

"That was before you and I connected. You can't hold that against me." He frowned.

"No, it wasn't before. It was earlier today. Before lunch. I heard you and I heard how desperate you sounded." I blinked back tears, then shook my head. "I get it. I understand why you're still hung up on her. I don't blame you if you're still in love with her. But why would you lie to me? How can you say that you care about me one second and lie through your teeth the next?"

"I'm not lying." He reached for my hands.

I jerked them away and leaned against the back door of the building. "You wanted her to be honest with you, right? If she had just told you that she wanted to see other people, you would have been able to get over that. But she didn't. She conned you. She kept you waiting in the wings while she had fun with a new guy. I know that had to hurt. I know it did, because it's the same thing that you've done to me." I turned the knob on the door and glared at him. "I'm no one's good time, Ollie. I will never be that. Good luck with Shauna, I honestly hope it works out, but you aren't going to ruin my life in the meantime."

"Maby, you don't understand!" He reached for me again.

"You're right, I don't." I stepped out of his reach, through

138

the back door, then pointed my finger at him. "Do not follow me. Do you understand me?"

"Please."

"Don't!" I glared at him. "If you follow me, I'll report you to the principal and to security and you'll get sent back to England far earlier than you planned."

"Maby, this is crazy!"

"I've warned you. If you take one step in my direction, I'm going straight to the principal's office. I'm not going to be toyed with. You had me on your hook, but I wiggled free, so just let me go." I started to close the door.

"Listen to me!" He lunged toward me, but the door closed before he could reach me.

Then I ran. I wasn't afraid of him. I knew that he wouldn't hurt me. I was afraid that if he caught me, I would give in to what I really wanted and kiss him.

Kiss him, despite everything that I knew to be true, despite the fact that he would never actually feel about me the way that I had to finally admit I felt about him. I needed to be as far from him as possible so that my brain would have time to rewire itself. I would not risk being any more hurt than I already was and I certainly would not risk losing any more friendships.

When I reached my dorm room, I slammed the door closed and locked it.

"Maby?" Fifi glanced up from the book she held, her eyes wide. "What's going on? Is something wrong?"

"No!" I gulped as I realized I'd shouted. "No, nothing is wrong anymore. Everything is just fine." I walked past her into my bedroom.

"Maby, I've never seen you like this." She followed me into my room and paused just inside the door. "What's wrong?"

"Nothing, like I said. I needed to end things with Oliver and

I did." I took a shaky breath as I met her eyes. "It's for the best. I need you to agree with me."

"If you say it's for the best, then I believe you." She walked over to me. "But that doesn't mean it won't hurt." She hugged me. "I'm so sorry you're going through this."

"Me too." I sighed as I rested my head on her shoulder and wrapped my arms around her. "I never thought this would happen to me."

"It happens to everyone eventually." She squeezed me, then took a step back to look at me. "If you want to talk about it, I'm willing to listen."

"I know. I just can't." I sank down onto my bed and clasped my hands together. "I need to detox from anything Oliver. Can you help me with that?"

"I'll do my best." She sat down beside me. "I'll keep him away from you and I'll never speak in an English accent, I promise."

"Don't make promises you can't keep." I smiled, despite the heaviness in my chest and the tears that welled up in my eyes.

I was lucky to have Fifi and all my other friends. For the first time since Jenny had left, I could see that. Unfortunately, it didn't erase the hurt that made my entire body ache.

"I'm going to make us some popcorn, put a movie on, and get the ice cream out of the freezer." Fifi gave my knee a light slap. "Don't worry, we'll have this boy off your back before you ever have to see him again."

"How?" I looked up at her helplessly.

"The same way any girl gets over a boy. We'll watch movies with hot Hollywood actors that will make us forget all about—oh—oh, what was his name? Never mind." She winked at me, then headed out into the kitchen.

I closed my eyes and hoped that she would be right. I didn't know how long I could tolerate the racing thoughts that took over my brain. I didn't want to think about him, but the more I tried not to, the more I wondered where he was, what he might be doing, and when I might see him again.

He's a liar, Maby. A liar and in love with someone else. Let him go.

A small part of me regretted closing the door in his face. Maybe if I'd let him talk, he could have given me an explanation that I could understand.

I pushed the possibility away from my mind. It would have just been another lie.

TWENTY-FIVE

The next morning when I woke up for class, getting out of bed was the last thing that I wanted to do. I wished I could just stay hidden away in my room forever. But after a few minutes of entertaining the possibility, a different idea crossed my mind.

What if I didn't hide? What if I didn't feel bad at all? What if I didn't give him the satisfaction of knowing that he'd broken my heart?

I pushed my blanket off and onto the floor. I stepped into the shower and took a little extra time to enjoy the flow of the hot water. I imagined washing every one of his touches from my skin, from my hair, from my mind. The more I visualized it, the more free I felt.

Fifi had been right. The movies full of bright-eyed boys that always treated the girl right in the end had made me feel less dependent on Oliver. There were other boys out there. And more importantly, I had plenty of time to find them.

When I wiped the mirror clean and looked at my reflection, I renewed my promise to myself that I would not be distracted by anything. My future was waiting for me and I wanted to be part of it, not stuck in the past, shedding tears over a boy who never really cared in the first place.

Still, I applied a little extra make-up and took a little more time on my hair. I wanted to look my best—not to attract a new love interest and not even to make Oliver feel jealous, but because I wanted to show off my pride in myself. Whether he intended to do it or not, he had broken my heart, but I wouldn't let that show.

As I pulled on my school uniform, I repeated a mantra in my mind. *I am more than enough. I am worthy of being happy.*

It was a mantra that I'd heard my mother say many times growing up. No matter what difficulty she faced, she would recite those words and her face would light up with confidence. I hoped that mine did the same. Although we didn't always agree on everything, I was glad for the lessons she'd taught me about self-esteem and independence.

I was almost to my first class when one of the teachers' aides caught me in the hall.

"Maby, I've been trying to get a message to you. You're needed in the administration office."

"I am? For what?" I frowned.

"I'm not sure, but I'd get there fast." He nodded to me, then hurried down the hall.

I sighed as I changed direction. The last thing I needed at the moment was trouble. I wracked my mind in an attempt to figure out why I might be summoned to the office.

When I pulled open the door to the administration building, I smelled it. Vanilla and lilacs. My mother's favorite perfume. I followed the scent right to the reception area where I saw her standing there, phone in hand.

"Mom?" I stared at her. "What are you doing here?"

"You don't remember? I told you I'd be here today." She

crossed her arms as she studied me. "Mabel, have you been eating? You look a bit thin."

"I'm fine, Mom, I promise." I gazed at her, then shook my head. "I'm sorry, I forgot all about your visit. I've been distracted."

"Distracted?" She raised an eyebrow. "By what?" She leaned closer to me. "It better not be a boy."

"It's not a boy, Mom." I rolled my eyes. "It's just been a rough week."

"I'm sorry to hear that." She hugged me. "Well, the important thing is that we're together now. I'm going to take you out for lunch and we'll do a little shopping. I can't stay as long as I originally planned. I have to catch a flight to Paris in a few hours."

"Paris?" I brightened at the thought. "Can I go with you? I promise, I won't be any trouble."

"Of course not." She quirked an eyebrow. "You have school, Maby."

"Please, Mom?" I stared into her eyes. "I really need a break."

"From what?" She laughed as she waved at the pile of laundry being rolled past us to be delivered to individual rooms. "All of the luxury you have here?"

"I could really use a little getaway. I've had good grades this year, I haven't been in any trouble. Can't I come?" My heart pounded as I hoped she would agree. Oliver certainly couldn't follow me to Paris.

"I'm sorry, hon, but that's just not possible. We can go this summer, though—you and me—we'll make it a girls' week, okay?" She looped her arm through mine. "Now let's go eat. I'm starving."

As disappointment washed over me, I held back what I thought of her decision. My mother had always put school above everything, as if it was the most important thing in the world. But at the moment, I wanted to be as far from Oak Brook Academy as possible.

As I walked with her to the gate, I noticed a strange tingling sensation on the back of my neck. I glanced over my shoulder to see what it might be and found Oliver at the entrance of the administration building. He had a pink suitcase in one hand and his phone in the other.

As I watched, a girl emerged from the administration building. She couldn't be more perfect if she tried, from perfectly styled hair to a fit and sexy body. She looked like a model. But she wasn't a model. I narrowed my eyes as I realized exactly who she was.

Shauna.

Of course I had no way to know for sure if it was her. At least not until she threw her arms around Oliver's neck and planted a heavy kiss on his lips.

"Oh my!" My mother clucked her tongue as she watched them. "That poor girl, she's going to get herself into quite a mess with that boy. Look at him, all hands." She huffed, then narrowed her eyes as she looked back at me. "You're lucky, Mabel, you know that?"

"I am?" I turned away as Oliver finally broke the kiss. "How?" I stepped through the gate, with my mother right beside me.

"You don't have to worry about any of that nonsense. You've always been too smart for that. I only wish your friend Jenny had been as smart." She pursed her lips, then shook her head. "Every time I hear something about her mother, I feel so bad for her."

"What? Why?" I glanced at her as we continued to walk along the sidewalk.

"Why? Because her daughter had such a bright future and

they've had to hide her away for almost a year. She lost so many friends." She scrunched up her nose. "I really think their idea of sending her back to Oak Brook Academy is terrible."

"She's coming back?" My eyes widened at the thought. "I didn't know you were in touch with her mother."

"Yes, I spoke to her after I found out. I let her know it would be best that you and Jenny didn't communicate. She understood." She frowned. "I know it's not her mother's fault, but I just have to wonder, what did she teach Jenny? Didn't she warn her to be careful? Or to stay away from boys altogether?"

"Wait." I stopped in the middle of the sidewalk. "Are you saying that you told Jenny's mother to keep her away from me?"

"Oh, I wasn't the only one. Everyone told her the same thing. I think that's why they sent Jenny off to her aunt in Alabama. In my opinion, they should have left her there. It would give her a fresh start. But she's been fighting to get Jenny back into Oak Brook. Such a scandal." She sucked her teeth, then signaled for a taxi. "I'm so glad you've never given me that kind of trouble. You're such a good girl, Mabel."

TWENTY-SIX

As the taxi pulled up, I thought my mind might explode. Never once had I imagined that Jenny might think I didn't want to speak to her. Never once had it crossed my mind that she might have been the one that felt abandoned.

"I'm not going anywhere with you." I stepped back from the taxi.

"Nonsense, get in the taxi." My mother frowned. "I told you, I don't have much time."

"No. You had no right to do that to Jenny." I glared at her as I started back along the sidewalk. "Go to Paris, go to the moon for all I care—I can't even look at you right now!"

"Mabel, you're being unreasonable!" she called after me.

As tears streaked down my cheeks, I felt too dizzy to make sense of where I was going. Had Jenny believed that I wanted nothing to do with her this whole time? Had she gone through the most difficult experience in her life believing that she was completely alone? The force of the horror I felt over that threatened to knock me off my feet.

Still blinded by my tears, I ran in no specific direction. I ran away from sound, away from anyone who might see me. I ran mostly from the truth that my mother had just revealed to me and the memory of Oliver kissing Shauna. Not long before, my life had been exactly as it should be, from top to bottom. Now, it felt as if I had shattered into thousands of pieces, such tiny shards that they could never be retrieved. Nothing felt possible anymore, not the future I once thought I wanted, not even my next breath.

I slammed into something solid and warm, with arms that wrapped around me. As a pulse of fear jolted me from the chaos in my mind, I recognized the eyes that locked to mine, the lips that brushed across my forehead, and the scent of the body that held me close.

"Ollie."

"Sh." He pressed my head into his chest as he held me.

I could hear the sound of his heartbeat. I could feel the tremor in his muscles as he held me tighter than anyone ever had before. Somewhere beneath my grief and shock, anger bubbled up. It demanded that I wrench myself free from his grasp. But the tears that flowed from my eyes and the exhaustion that caused my entire body to ache kept me right where I was.

More than anything at that moment, I needed to know that I wasn't alone. I needed to remember what it was like when he looked at me, when he touched me, when he whispered my name beside my ear, and when he uttered soft reassurances.

"I've got you, Maby." He pushed his lips through my hair until they tickled the ridge of my ear. "I've got you, I'm right here."

His words inspired even more tears to flow, as they were the sweetest words I'd ever heard in my entire life. I had no idea how much I longed for them until I heard them and then I wondered how I'd survived without them.

I clung to him as he guided me down onto a bench. His fingers trailed through my hair, smoothing it away from my face.

I could feel the sunlight strike the moisture on my skin. How could it be so bright out? How could the weather not reflect the torment that I felt?

As I opened my eyes, I looked right into his. The memory of his kissing Shauna flashed through my mind, but just then, I didn't care. I didn't care who he might have been kissing, who he might be in love with, who he might be using me to forget. All I cared about was his hands as they wrapped around mine and the softness of his voice as he spoke.

"You don't have to talk about it. You don't have to say a word." He released one of my hands and ran his fingertips along the tears that still flowed.

As he wiped them away, more threatened to form. I'd never felt so completely lost in my emotions. I knew that I hated him, but I couldn't imagine asking him to stop.

He pressed his lips against my forehead. Then he left a light kiss at the corner of my eye. He placed another on the rise of my cheekbone, then on the tender skin of my cheek. As his chin brushed against my lips, my heartbeat rocketed to a level I'd never experienced before.

Yes, I thought, *yes, please just kiss me. Please just make something wonderful happen to combat all this chaos.*

His lips hovered there, at the corner of mine, as if seeking permission to slide just a little closer.

All I had to do was turn my head—not even a full turn, just the smallest tilt to the side—and our lips would meet. All I had to do was take what I wanted—demand it. But just as I started the movement, a rush of fury broke through the fog of grief that had driven all logic from my mind.

"Maby." His forehead glided along mine as he sensed my movement and sought my lips.

"Don't." I ducked away just before our lips could touch. One word wasn't enough to contain the anger that erupted from me. "Don't you dare!" I shoved his shoulders so hard that he nearly fell off the bench.

He caught himself on the back of it and gazed at me with wide eyes. "I'm sorry, I thought it was what you wanted."

I pushed myself up from the bench as I glared at him. "Of course it's what I want!"

"I don't understand." He stood up from the bench as well but remained a short distance from me. "Maby, if you would just give me a chance to explain."

"No, no more chances." I wiped my palms across my cheeks, not just to clear away the remainder of my tears, but to remove the memory of his kisses. "You came into my life, you forced your way into my life. You filled my head with lies and all of these ridiculous feelings!"

"They're not ridiculous and they're not lies." He grabbed my hand and held it tight as I tried to pull it away. "Just listen to me!"

"No!" I grabbed his wrist and wrenched his hand free as I stared into his eyes. "I won't listen! It's your turn to listen! I may be nothing to you, but I still exist! You toyed with me for your own entertainment to make yourself feel better. I'm sorry that Shauna broke your heart, I'm sorry that she cheated on you, but that doesn't give you the right to get your revenge on me! I was fine!" I pushed his hand away as he tried to grab mine again. "I was fine until you showed up! Now look at me!" I drew a sharp breath as my mind spun with dizziness. "I'm a mess!"

As I stumbled, he caught me by the elbow to steady me and for an instant our bodies leaned against each other.

As I pulled away, I accidentally looked into his eyes and there it was again, the urge to kiss him.

"Of course I want to kiss you. Of course it's what I want."

With his hand still on my elbow, he guided me back toward him and in one swift movement his lips brushed against mine.

"No!" I shoved him away before the kiss could become more than a graze. "Don't you see? It doesn't matter what I want!" I glared at him. "It's not what you want. I'm not who you want." I gasped as the weight of the entire day threatened to crush me. "If you ever cared about me at all, even a little bit, you would walk away right now."

TWENTY-SEVEN

"Maby." His eyes locked to mine.

"Just go!" I turned away from him as fresh tears began to flow. "Please!"

"I can't do that." His hands ran along the curves of my shoulders in a gentle caress, then held them. "I won't!"

"Because it's more important that you get what you want, right?" I turned back to face him. "Because all you care about is you."

He narrowed his eyes as he looked at me. "Because you're the most important thing to me and I'm not going to walk away unless I know that you're okay."

"Why do you keep telling lies?" I balled my hands into fists. "Why can't you just admit the truth? You made a mistake. You thought you could move on by distracting yourself with me, but you couldn't. Why can't you just say that to me, instead of pretending that things are different?"

"Because that's not the truth." He frowned. "If you would give me a chance to explain, you would know that."

"I'm not going to give you a chance to con me again. Never."

JILLIAN ADAMS

I held up my hands and backed away from him. "You've done enough damage here."

"I'm sorry, Maby." His expression softened. "I'm sorry. I never meant to cause you any pain, I promise you that. I never wanted to do anything more than be the person that you need, that you deserve. But things have gotten a little mixed up."

"I don't call kissing Shauna a little mixed up." I made a sound that should have been a laugh, but it came out too harsh to be described that way. "I call it you playing both sides and seeing which one you like better."

"You saw that?" His face paled. "I didn't know."

"Of course you didn't. You didn't know that you got caught in the act, otherwise you wouldn't have wasted so much time pretending to be something you're not."

"That's not what happened." He stepped in front of me as I tried to move past him. "Listen to me, Maby! Just for one second, listen to me!"

"I don't want to! Aren't you hearing me? I'm already embarrassed enough. Just go back to her, just move on with your life. Please!" I stepped around him before he could stop me, but his hand caught mine and pulled me back.

"I am not with Shauna!" He locked his eyes to mine. "Do you hear me? I'm not with her!"

"I just saw you kissing her!" My heart skipped a beat, despite my anger. Could he be telling me the truth?

"She kissed me." He frowned. "And you're right, I shouldn't have let it happen, but it was so sudden that it took me by surprise." He sighed, then shook his head. "But I'm glad it did happen."

"I'm sure you are." I narrowed my eyes.

"I'm glad because it proved to me one hundred percent that there is nothing left between Shauna and me. It disappeared the

156

moment I met you." He licked his lips, then closed his eyes. "When I spoke to her on the phone—what you heard—it was me pleading with her not to come here. She'd decided she wanted me back and planned this reunion for us. I asked her not to come, but she'd already bought the ticket and was at the airport. She wouldn't listen to me." He opened his eyes again and looked at me. "Once, I begged her to come back to me. But when she decided she would, I didn't want her to anymore, because I'd fallen for you." He tightened his grasp on my hand. "Whether you believe me or not, it doesn't change how I feel. I love you, Maby."

Those words struck me hard. One by one, they took my breath away.

He loved me? My heartbeat quickened. No boy had ever said that to me before. No one had even come close. For an instant, I thought my feet weren't even touching the ground anymore. If it was true—if he was over Shauna and in love with me—could I tell him the truth? Could I admit that I was in love with him too?

I opened my mouth to say those words. I felt my body tilt forward, ready to be swept up in his arms. I wanted more than anything to taste his lips for the first time. But just as I was about to speak, I recalled Jenny's infectious laugh. I remembered the girl she was before she'd gotten involved with a boy, before she'd lost herself in the very emotions that I felt driving me toward Oliver.

"Ollie." His name slipped past as my mouth grew dry.

"Maby, I need you to believe me." He cupped my cheeks and looked into my eyes. "Can you do that?"

"Yes." I whispered the word. "But it doesn't matter."

"What do you mean it doesn't matter? She means nothing to me. I promise. You can trust me." He smoothed his thumbs along my still damp cheeks. "Let's just let it flow, right? Like we planned? You don't have to say it back, not yet, not if you don't want to."

"No." I wrapped around his wrists and pulled his hands from my face. "I'm sorry, Ollie, but no."

"No?" He stared at me, then his eyes widened. "Maby, don't do this. I know you have feelings for me too. Don't do this!"

"It doesn't matter." I let my hands fall back to my sides. "None of this does. We're just kids. We're too young for any of it."

"Don't say that." His voice roughened with desperation. "I know what I feel about you is real and I know what you feel for me is real too. Don't be so scared that you make both of us miss out on something so amazing."

"You knew you felt this way about Shauna too, didn't you?" I took a step back, my mind in a daze from the endless emotions that I'd cycled through. "You begged for her to take you back, because you thought she was the one, your true love."

"I didn't know any better!" He frowned as he reached for me.

"No!" I took another step back. "I won't do this. I won't sacrifice my life, my future, my plans, because of some crazy hormones or a bout of loneliness. This part of my life doesn't happen now. It happens in college, with two years of my studies under my belt and a man who will understand the importance of my career. It happens with someone who isn't just out of a break-up, who isn't from another continent, who doesn't have to beg me to stay."

"You're making a mistake, Maby." He sunk his hands in his hair and tugged at the roots as he groaned. "You're so caught up in what you think is right and wrong that you're going to destroy us both."

"No." I shook my head as I studied him. "I'm saving us both from making a huge mistake. If you want to be in love so badly,

Ollie, then go back to Shauna. Love her. Even though she made a mistake, love her anyway. She'll love you back."

"Not like you." His lips drew into a tight line as he studied me. "You can deny it all you want, but I see something in your eyes when you look at me, something that I never saw in hers."

"I'm sorry." I turned away from him. "Good luck, Ollie, good luck with everything."

"I'm not the one walking away!" He called out to me as I walked off. "Remember that, Maby, I'm still standing right here!"

I closed my eyes tight and took a shaky breath as I fought the urge to turn and race right back into his arms. Instead, I forced one foot in front of the other until I found myself in my dorm room with the door locked and my head buried in my pillow. Yes, it would hurt for a little while, but in the end I would be fine.

I knew I was right.

TWENTY-EIGHT

The next few days went by in a blur. I managed to avoid running into Oliver while also dodging phone calls and texts from my mother. I had no idea how to even speak to her after the betrayal I felt.

While my friends tried to get the truth out of me, I kept my distance from them too. With the raging storm that had formed inside me, I didn't trust myself to be around anyone.

With each day that passed, I guessed that Oliver was one day closer to going back to England. Then I might finally get some relief from the constant pressure that had settled in my chest. Despite my avoidance of him, I still woke each morning wondering when I might see him again and hoping to hear his voice.

On Saturday morning when I woke up, I could feel the faint graze of his lips against mine. A rush of excitement carried through me as I opened my eyes, expecting to see him.

Instead, only my bedroom ceiling stared back at me. That pressure in my chest became a crushing weight that made it difficult for me to breathe.

"Ollie." I closed my eyes again and wished that I could fall back into a deep sleep. If I could just get through the next few weeks, I knew that I'd be okay. At least I hoped that I would be. As I tried to push away all memories of him, I decided to go for a ride. It would help me to clear my head and maybe fill it with fantasies of Aaron again.

Safe Aaron. Aaron, whom I could never actually have a relationship with. Aaron, who only wanted to teach me how to ride horses. I didn't have to worry about him touching my cheek or grabbing my hand. He wouldn't have a problem with me walking away.

I licked my lips as the memory of those last intoxicating moments with Oliver filled my mind. All I wanted to do was turn back, to let him pull me right into his arms. But I knew better than to give in to that desire.

I took a deep breath as I looked in the mirror. "I should be proud of myself, really." I gazed at my reflection. "I used self-control. I resisted. One day, I'd meet the right person and I'd be so glad that I'd waited."

I smiled, but even I wasn't convinced by it. Usually those words would give me a burst of confidence and enthusiasm. Today, they only left me feeling more alone.

What if I had met the right person? What if he'd just come a little earlier than I'd planned? What if he was telling the truth about being over Shauna and I'd pushed him away?

I shook my head, ignoring the what-ifs as I dressed to go to the stables. With no storms in the forecast, I felt fairly safe to ride on my own, but I didn't plan to turn down the option of Aaron riding with me.

In the taxi on the way to the stables I tried to imagine my life without Oliver in it. Soon, he would just be a memory.

I stepped out of the taxi and walked up the driveway toward the stables. As soon as I heard the horses, a wave of peace washed over me. Maybe I could leave behind my troubles just for a little while.

As I led Goldie out of her stall, I spotted Aaron in one of the corrals. He had the reins of a horse in his hand and he was looking up at a girl perched on the horse. Her long dark hair fell in thick curls to her shoulders as she threw her head back and laughed.

The sound of the laughter nearly knocked me off my feet. It couldn't be possible. Could it? My heart raced as I watched her coax the horse forward, her back still to me.

It had to be my imagination. I took a few steps toward the corral, my mind still fogged by the familiarity of the laugh I heard.

"Take it slow, you'll get used to it again real fast." Aaron smoothed his hand along the horse's mane and smiled up at the girl on the horse. "It's good to see you back here."

"It's good to be back." The girl tilted her head back to look at the sky, then nodded. "Or at least, almost back."

Her voice, her hair, her laugh. I found myself at the fence, my mouth half-open.

"Oh, Mabel, I didn't know you were coming out today." Aaron flashed me a smile. "Just give me a few minutes, unless you want to ride together?" He looked up at the girl on the horse. "Like old times?"

"Jenny?" I whispered her name as she turned to look at me. Those sea-blue eyes locked to mine and then looked quickly away.

"No, I'm sure she'd rather ride alone, Aaron. Can we get started?"

"Jenny!" I tried to get through the gate of the corral, but Goldie decided to be stubborn.

"I'm just here for a ride, Maby. I'm not going to cause any trouble." She looked back at me, her lips tightened into a frown.

"Or are you going to tell your mother to get me kicked out of here too?"

"I would never do that!" I tied Goldie's reins to the fence of the corral and made my way through the gate.

"I thought that too." She took the reins of the horse from Aaron's hand. "But it turns out I was wrong."

"Jenny, I've been trying to reach you this whole time! Have you gotten any of my e-mails?" I walked toward her.

"Just stop, Maby. You thought you'd never have to see me again, so it didn't matter how cruel you were. But it turns out, I'm here." She smirked as she studied me. "Not what you thought either, huh? I can handle a lot more than you thought possible. Now, if you don't mind, I want to go for a ride." She turned her horse, guided him to one end of the corral, then urged him into a gallop.

"Jennifer, don't!" Aaron shouted at her as the horse charged toward the other end of the corral. "Stop right now!"

"Jenny, be careful!" I gasped as I saw the horse launch itself into the air. Despite the fear that rocketed through me, I couldn't look away from the beauty of the horse as it sailed over the fence, with Jennifer's long hair trailing behind them. The horse landed on the other side and continued at its fast pace toward the trail.

"Doesn't anyone listen to me?" Aaron pulled off his hat and threw it on the ground. "I should ban her!"

"Don't." I picked up his hat and dusted it off. "Please, Aaron." I offered it back to him. "It's my fault she did that."

"Is it?" He looked into my eyes as he took his hat from me. "Because from where I stand, it seems like you were trying to be her friend."

"I was, I always was." I bit into my bottom lip as I watched her disappear down the trail. "But she doesn't know that."

"Mabel." He put his hand on my shoulder as he studied me.

"Are you okay? It seems like you've had a rough time lately. Something is different about you."

As Aaron focused all his attention on me, I realized that I'd dreamed about the moment a million times. The moment that Aaron finally noticed me. The moment that he showed how much he cared about me. It should have filled me with excitement and passion. Instead, I only saw a teacher who wanted to help me.

"I'm okay." I forced a smile. "It has been a little rough. But I'm okay."

"Good. Just hang in there." He smiled. "High school isn't forever, you know. Before you know it, it'll all be over and you'll be free to do whatever you want."

"Thanks." His words settled into my mind.

"Let's get you out there for a ride. I'm sure that will help." He walked with me back to Goldie.

As he made sure she was ready to go out on the trail, I felt my affection for him transform from an impossible crush into a genuine appreciation. He'd taught me more than just horseback riding. He'd taught me to look beyond the moment, to believe in the future. But could I look forward to a future without Jenny or Oliver in it?

TWENTY-NINE

As I guided Goldie down the trail ahead of me, I listened for the sound of other hoofbeats. Seeing Jennifer again had been quite a shock. But now that I'd had time to adjust to it, I had one goal. I wanted to speak to her. I wanted to tell her that I'd never meant to abandon her. However, I didn't hear anyone behind me.

I turned Goldie toward another path, a path that Jennifer and I had followed many times together. As I urged the horse along the trail, my mind spun with questions. I wanted to know everything that Jennifer had been through over the past year and what she might be planning for her future. More than anything, I wanted her to forgive me.

"Looking for me?"

I looked up at a branch that stretched over the trail above me and saw two bare feet dangling down.

"Jenny, what are you doing up there?"

"Waiting for you." She tipped her head toward her horse. "There's a good tree over there and a stream where Goldie can get a drink. Tie her and climb up."

I frowned as I slid down out of the saddle. I wasn't sure if I wanted to climb up on a tree branch, but I did know that I wanted the chance to speak to her. After Goldie was secure, I walked over to the tree and looked up at Jennifer.

"I'm so glad to see you."

"Sure." She rolled her eyes.

"Jenny, I mean it. I've missed you so much." I eyed the tree a few moments longer, then began to climb it. The higher I got, the more nervous I became, but I was determined not to back down. I swung my leg over the thick tree branch and scooted out toward her. "I had no idea you were here."

"No one does. Well, almost no one." She sighed as she looked at the trees in the distance. "I thought I'd take a ride while everything gets sorted out. Get my mind off of things."

"How are you?" I placed my hand over hers and looked into her eyes.

"How am I?" She laughed as she pulled her hand away. Only it was not the laugh that I remembered. It wasn't jovial. It was dark and bitter.

"Please." I frowned as I studied her. "I know that you don't believe me, but I had no idea what my mother did. I have tried to reach you. Your number was disconnected and you never answered any of my e-mails. I thought you were just done with me."

"You thought I was done with you?" She peered at me. "I needed you, Maby. You were my best friend."

"I know that, and I know I wasn't there for you at first—not the way that I should have been—but I wanted to be. One day you were here, the next you were gone, and I tried to find you." I searched her eyes. "I swear I did. I've worried about you and wondered about how you were—and about the baby." I swallowed hard as I said the word.

"Ah, at least you're brave enough to say it. Most people act like the baby didn't even exist." She brushed her hand lightly over her stomach, then frowned. "She's okay."

"A girl?" I smiled as I looked at her.

"Yes, a girl." She shrugged and looked down at her bare toes. "I didn't find out until she was born."

"You wanted to be surprised?"

"No, I just didn't want to know." She tipped her head to the side as she looked over at me. "You really didn't know what your mother did?"

"I didn't, Jenny." I took her hand and squeezed it. "I had no idea. Not until a few days ago. She told me that she told your mother not to let you communicate with me. But I never wanted that. I wanted to be there for you."

"I figured you probably didn't want to talk to me—since I disappointed you." She looked down at my hand holding hers, then back up at me.

"What do you mean you disappointed me?"

"I made a mistake and it ruined everything." She pursed her lips, then glanced away. "I really messed up."

"Jenny, I know I was hard on you when you first told me about it." I chewed on my bottom lip. "I was terrible."

"You weren't wrong."

"I was wrong." I scooted closer to her and the branch beneath us creaked. "I get it now. I honestly didn't then, but I get it now. I get how you can be so caught up in a feeling that it doesn't even feel like you have a choice to make."

"You do?" She met my eyes. "How?"

Oliver's face flashed through my mind. I gripped the branch beneath me and closed my eyes.

"I met someone."

"You?" Her eyes widened. "The great and powerful Maby whose rules shall never be broken?"

"It's not funny." I sighed. "I feel terrible for the way I treated you."

"Don't." Her voice softened. "You were the only person that

had my back. I know that now. When my parents sent me to live with my Aunt Jasmine, I thought my life was over. Then I discovered that she had gotten rid of her Internet. My parents didn't want me to have any chance of connecting with my friends. So no, I didn't get any of your e-mails. I didn't even have a phone."

"That must have been awful." I narrowed my eyes.

"Not as awful as other things, but it wasn't fun, that's for sure. It gave me a lot of time to think—to really focus on what was coming next."

"What did come next?" I lowered my voice. "If you don't mind my asking."

"I don't want to talk about it. Not right now." She looked up at me and smiled, that familiar, amazing smile that I'd missed so much. "I want to talk about this person you met. What's his name?"

"It doesn't matter." I sighed as I looked up at the sky.

"Why not?" She frowned.

"It's over now." I shrugged. "It was a bad idea from the start and now it's over."

"Wait a minute. Are you saying that someone broke through the fortress of Maby and you're letting that person go?"

"It's more complicated than that."

"Is it?" She searched my eyes. "Because I know how determined you were not to have feelings for anyone in high school. So, if this guy managed to break through those barriers, then he must be pretty fantastic."

"Fantastic or not, it's over." I clenched my jaw, then shook my head. "We should get down from here before Aaron comes looking for us."

"Like you would mind that." She grinned.

"Eh." I shrugged. "I'm not that into him anymore."

"What?" She laughed as she followed me down the trunk of

the tree. "Now I really have to meet this guy. I didn't think you'd ever get over your crush on Aaron."

"A crush?" Aaron pulled his horse to a stop as we both turned to face him. "Who has a crush on Aaron?"

Mortified, my cheeks flushed as his eyes met mine. It had never crossed my mind that he might find out or that I might be face to face with him when he did.

"I know it can't be you, Mabel." He smiled at me as he slid down off his horse.

THIRTY

I could barely take a breath as Aaron walked toward me.

"Oh, it's nothing." I forced a smile.

"I'm sure it is." He crossed his arms as he looked between us. "I don't want there to be a problem here. I'm your teacher, nothing more."

"We know that." I cleared my throat as I glanced over at Jennifer.

"Sure we do." She shrugged. "We were just joking around."

"I thought you must be. After I saw you with Oliver the other day, I assumed the two of you were dating." Aaron raised an eyebrow. "Not that it's any of my business."

"Oh, Oliver, huh?" Jennifer grinned as she looked at me. "Now I know."

"Never mind!" I groaned. "Just drop it."

"As for you, Jennifer..." Aaron settled his gaze on her. "One more crazy stunt like that and I'll be forced to ask you not to come back."

"Wouldn't be the first time." Jennifer rolled her eyes. "It seems like anything and anyone associated with Oak Brook wants nothing to do with me."

"You're the one that broke the rules." He narrowed his eyes. "It's not safe for you or the horse. All I ask from my students is respect for themselves and respect for the animals. Are you going to be able to provide that?"

"I'll do my best." She nodded. "I'm sorry."

"Good." He glanced up at the sky, then looked back at us. "Don't stay out too long, that sun is brutal today." He climbed back onto his horse, then nodded toward us. "Have fun."

"Have fun." Jennifer gave me a light shove as Aaron rode off. "Oh my gosh, that was crazy wasn't it?"

"Crazy doesn't begin to cover it." I leaned back against a tree and closed my eyes. "Could you imagine if he found out the truth? It doesn't matter now anyway. I don't have a crush on him anymore."

"What?" Her eyes widened. "You've had a crush on him since we both started at Oak Brook Academy.

"I know." I shrugged. "It was always just for fun and now it's just not fun anymore."

"Because of Oliver?"

"Because I'm growing up." I crossed my arms. "Because none of it is real anyway."

"What isn't real?"

"Love." I shrugged. "I guess."

"Oh, Maby, someone has really done something to hurt you, huh?" She took my hand in hers and sighed. "I really thought you might get out of high school unscathed."

"I guess not." I blinked my eyes as tears started to form. "Maby, I really have missed you so much. You have no idea how many times I wanted to talk to you—needed to talk to you."

"It was the same for me." She smiled some. "At least now I know that you don't hate me. That makes me feel a lot better."

"I could never hate you." I squeezed her hand. "Never."

"I'm here now. Why don't you talk to me?" She led me over

to a soft patch of grass. "Let's hash it all out. Let's get to the bottom of it."

"I'm not sure that I can even think about it anymore." I pressed my hand against my chest. "It hurts so much."

"That pain is something that's not going to go away."

"That is not helpful." I groaned.

"I know, I'm sorry." She sat down beside me. "But it's the truth. You know I won't lie to you, Maby. When I left Oak Brook, it hurt, a lot. I thought maybe he would make an effort to see me, to check on me at least, but he didn't. Not a word."

"Oh, Jenny, I'm sorry." I wrapped my arm around her shoulders. "I can't believe that you had to go through all this alone."

"To be honest, I wasn't exactly alone. I relied a lot on our talks to help me get through it. All the advice that you've given me over the years. Of course, it hurt to think of you too." She pushed her hair back from her face and sighed. "It's been rough. I can't deny that. But coming back here—seeing you again—it's given me back a bit of hope."

"I'm glad." I smiled. "I'm so happy that you're coming back."

"Well, I'm not back yet. But my parents sure are trying. They want me to have the best education and that means Oak Brook Academy." She ran her fingertips through the grass. "Right now, I'm here. Who knows what tomorrow will bring? But while I'm here, I want to know—what can I do to bring back that spark in your eye?"

"What spark?"

"The spark I saw the moment that Aaron said the name Oliver."

"Ugh." I closed my eyes. "That's over. It's too late to do anything about it now."

"The way your voice shakes when you say that makes me think that it's not over. Not even close. How long have you two been dating?"

"Not at all. You know my rule."

"Seriously?" She leaned her shoulder against mine. "I think you're going to have to give up on that rule, hon, because you've got it bad for this Oliver."

"No—no, I don't." I straightened my shoulders. "It was a mistake. One I don't intend to make again."

"If he made you that happy, then are you sure it was a mistake?"

"I can't risk it, Jen, you know that."

"All I know is that when I left here, you had zero interest in romance. Now that I'm back, you're denying yourself something that is probably the most magical experience you'll ever have." She rocked back on her heels. "Sure, we both had a lot of plans, but the one thing you can count on in life is that those plans will change. Mine had to and now maybe yours need to change too."

"That's exactly what shouldn't happen." I met her eyes as my muscles tensed. "I'm not going to let it happen. I'm going to stay in control. Soon enough, he'll go back to England and his ex and all of this will just be something that almost happened to me."

"Oh, honey." She slung her arm around my shoulders and squeezed. "It's already happening. The only question is, are you going to hide from it or are you going to explore it?"

"Hide." I smiled as I glanced over at her. "Absolutely, one hundred percent hide."

"We'll see." She raised an eyebrow.

"You don't believe me?"

"I know you a little better than you think. I've never seen you back down from a challenge. Hiding just isn't your way of handling things." She straightened up and crossed her arms. "Tell me I'm wrong."

"Maybe it isn't usually." I slid my hands into my pockets and let out a long breath. "But this time is different."

"I know it is." She lowered her voice as she leaned close to me. "This time you're scared."

"I'm not." I narrowed my eyes.

"Then why are you hiding your hands?" She smirked. "Maybe because they're shaking?"

"Jenny, you of all people should understand." I frowned. "No matter what I'm feeling, I've got to stay in control."

"I understand that no matter how much you want to be in control, sometimes you just don't have it." She shrugged. "You may not understand this, Maby, but I don't regret what happened. Do I wish the circumstances had been different? Sure. But the things that happen in life are just that—things that happen. When you make a mistake, most of the time the world doesn't come to an end. Buildings don't collapse, the sky doesn't fall." She placed her hands on my shoulders and looked into my eyes. "But the regret of the missed opportunity? The risk that you were too scared to take? That can haunt you."

"Jenny." I sighed as I turned away from her.

"I know, I know. I'm probably the last one that you want to take advice from."

"That's not true." I looked back at her. "Jenny, you're the only one I've wanted to talk to. I just don't know if this is a risk I can take."

THIRTY-ONE

"That's something only you can decide." Jennifer looked down the trail back toward the stables. "We really should get back. I managed to get a few hours free from my mother's supervision, but it's going to expire soon. I don't want to disrupt her good will." She frowned as she untied the reins of her horse.

"When are you coming back to Oak Brook?" I untied my horse's reins as well.

"I'm not sure yet. It's not definite." She climbed onto her horse. "It's a bit of a battle to get back in. Sometimes I think it isn't worth it."

"It is." I climbed onto Goldie and guided her along beside Jennifer's horse. "It absolutely is, Jenny. I can't wait to have you back. I'm so sorry it took us this long to reconnect."

"It's no one's fault." She offered a sad smile. "I'm glad we're together again too."

"Anything I can do to help get you back into Oak Brook, just let me know."

"Thanks, Maby. I appreciate that."

I left the stables with my thoughts swirling through my

mind. Not only was it amazing to see Jennifer again, but her advice had taken root inside of me.

When I arrived at Oak Brook, I felt Jennifer's absence as I walked through the gate. Hopefully, I wouldn't have to feel it much longer. My stomach twisted into a knot as I realized that there would be another absence that I'd be feeling soon. Would it be as heartbreaking?

I looked up just in time to see Oliver walking through the courtyard in my direction.

I froze at the sight of him. Distracted by Jennifer's presence, I'd forgotten to prepare myself for the possibility of running into Oliver. I needed to have my guard up, but I didn't.

It was too late. His eyes had already locked to mine. As he took each step toward me, I tried to will my feet to move in any direction that was away from him.

But when he paused in front of me, I still stood in the same spot.

"Maby." He tipped his head to the side. "I was beginning to wonder if you were still around."

"I'm here."

"I see that." He swept his gaze over me, then settled it on my eyes again. "Avoiding me then, I guess?"

"It seems like the right thing to do." I pushed my hair back over my shoulders, determined not to show the chaos that he inspired in me.

"How can it be right?" He squinted at me. "I don't think you believe that."

"How's Shauna?" I raised an eyebrow.

"She went back to England." He frowned as he glanced briefly away. "After I made it clear to her that things between us were over."

"You did?" My throat grew dry.

"Yes." His jaw tensed.

"That must have been hard for you." I noticed the strain in his eyes and the faint waver in his voice as he spoke.

"I never wanted to hurt her."

"Even after what she did to you?"

"Even after that." He shook his head. "She's not the one I'm angry with."

I bit into my bottom lip and looked down at the cobblestones between us.

"I should get to my dorm room." I started to step around him.

"Maby." His palm passed across my stomach as I moved past him. "Can't we talk?"

"There's nothing to talk about." I turned back to face him. "Is there?"

"I think so, yes." He shoved his hands into his pockets and narrowed his eyes. "Why are you still resisting this when I've shown you that I'm serious about what's between us?"

"Just because you want something to happen, that doesn't mean that I have to give in to it." I crossed my arms. "You don't get to dictate my emotions."

"I'm a dictator now?" He quirked an eyebrow as a faint smile tugged at his lips. "Is that what you think of me?"

"I think you keep pushing something that we've both agreed is not going to happen."

"I never agreed to that." His smile faded and was replaced by a stern glare. "I would never agree to that. All I'm asking is that you and I hash things out. Is that such a crazy idea? Like you said, I'm going back to England. It's what you want. But I'd like to leave with you as my friend."

"Friend?"

"You won't let me be anything else. You've made that very clear. But do we have to be enemies?" He took my hand. "I don't want it to be like that."

"Me either." I nodded as I studied him. "I'd like to be your friend."

"Maybe I pushed things too much." He held my hand a moment longer, then released it. "I want you to know that you can trust me. If you don't want to be with me, that's fine, but it doesn't change the fact that I'd like to get to know you better and maybe we can keep in touch."

"I'd like that." I felt some relief and also some disappointment as he smiled.

"Friends?" He met my eyes.

"Friends." I smiled in return.

"I hope that means that you don't have to avoid me anymore." He offered me his arm. "Why don't you join me for lunch?"

"Sure." I ignored the racing of my heartbeat as I wrapped my arm around his. "I'm starving."

"Me too." He grinned, then led me in the direction of the cafeteria.

I did my best to ignore the desire to pull him closer, to rest my head against his chest again. Luckily, I was so excited to tell my friends about seeing Jennifer that I managed to be distracted enough not to grab him by the collar and plant a kiss on him.

When we stepped into the cafeteria, Candy spotted us right away. I braced myself. Was she still angry with me?

"Over here!" She waved to us. "Hurry before all the cookies are gone."

"Cookies?" I sat down across from her.

"I made cookies." She smiled proudly. "I've decided that I'm going to be a chef."

"A chef?" I smiled. Candy tried out different future careers just about every week.

"Sure. But I'm not sure if I like baking or cooking more. So, I made the cookies today and tomorrow I'll whip up something else—to see which I like better."

"Isn't it possible to do both?" Oliver sat down beside me and picked up one of the cookies.

"Oh, great idea!" Candy smiled.

"If anyone can do it, you can." I picked up a cookie as well.

"I hope you like them." Candy leaned across the table and spoke softly to me. "I'm sorry about the other day. You know that, right?"

"I'm sorry too." I took a bite of the cookie. "Wow, this is delicious!"

"Thanks." She shrugged. "It's one of my grandmother's old recipes."

"It's great. You should definitely keep it in the mix."

"I will." She looked into my eyes. "I'm glad to see you two together. I think it's sweet."

"We're not together." I glanced at Oliver.

"Just friends." Oliver held up his hands.

"Ah, Maby's rules do still rule, huh?" Candy smiled. "You've got more self-control than me, that's for sure."

I squeezed my hands together underneath the table. If only that were true, I might not have had such a hard time focusing on anything other than Oliver sitting beside me.

"Guess who I saw today?"

"Who?" She leaned close.

"Jenny." The moment I said her name, a smile settled on my lips.

"Seriously?" Candy's eyes widened. "How is she? How's the baby?"

"She's okay. She's trying to come back to Oak Brook. Won't that be great?"

"Great." Candy frowned. "But do you really think they'll let her? You know how things are around here."

"I'm going to do everything I can to make sure they will."

"I might be able to help you out with that." Oliver glanced over at me. "Sorry for listening in, but I do have an in with the school board here. That's how I was able to just show up out of the blue. I should say that my dad has an in."

"You would do that?" I met his eyes. "You would help me?"

"I'd do anything to help you."

THIRTY-TWO

His words rippled through me, tickling my already sensitive nerves. As I looked into his eyes, I couldn't doubt that they were true.

"I'll make some calls later today." He stood up from the table. "I'll grab us some food before it's gone."

"I'd do anything." Candy swooned as she repeated Oliver's words and batted her eyes. "Oh, girl, he has it bad for you."

"I don't know about that." I frowned.

"What part do you doubt? The part where he sent his ex-girlfriend back to England or the part where he wants to be your friend even though you know he wants to be a lot more than that?" She plucked a fry from her plate, then popped it into her mouth.

"He just broke up with someone. I don't think it's even possible for him to be ready for someone new. He may think he is, but that's just the rebound talking." I stole one of her fries.

"And if it's not?" She frowned. "What if it's real?"

"How am I supposed to know?"

"Close your eyes." She dusted the salt from her hands then took a sip of her water.

"What?" I stared at her.

"I can help you figure it out. But you have to close your eyes." She looked over at the lunch line. "Hurry, before he comes back."

"Fine." I sighed, then closed my eyes.

"Now, I want you to imagine yourself all alone on an island."

"This is silly."

"It's not silly. Just imagine it." She gave my foot a nudge under the table.

"Okay. I'm all alone on an island." I envisioned a beautiful beach stretched out before me, edged with clear blue water. As I sunk my toes into the sand, I decided I might just want to stay there. "Now what?"

"Now, I want you to imagine someone walking up to you. The person is so far away, you can't really tell who it is."

"Okay." I frowned as I imagined a faint figure in the distance.

"As the person gets closer, you can see that it's Oliver."

Instantly my heartbeat quickened. I bit into my bottom lip.

"He's almost to you now. He's reaching his hand out to you. He's saying something that you can't quite hear."

Despite the noise of the cafeteria, I was only aware of Oliver's soft voice. I couldn't quite make out what he said, but just the sound of his words left me eager to hear more.

"Now he's gone." Candy snapped her fingers. "He's completely vanished."

My heart lurched, then dropped as the image of him disappeared. My eyes flew open and I took a sharp breath in the same moment that my fingernails dug into the palms of my hands.

"So? Is it real?" Candy's eyes locked to mine.

"Here you go." Oliver set a tray down in front of me.

I reached for his hand without even thinking about it and

the moment my fingertips grazed across his skin, my heart began to race.

"You okay?" He peered at me as I drew my hand away.

"Yes." I cleared my throat. "Thanks for this." I slid the tray closer to me.

"My pleasure." He turned his attention to Wes and began to chat about something in a class they shared.

I couldn't hear a single word he said over the pounding of my heart. I looked back at Candy and found a knowing smile on her lips.

Yes, it was real. More real than I could have ever imagined. More real than anything I'd ever experienced. I pushed my tray back and stood up from the table.

"I'm actually not very hungry."

"Are you sure?" Oliver looked up at me. "You didn't eat anything."

"I know—sorry, my stomach is a little upset." I backed away from the table.

"I'll walk you back to your room—to make sure you get there alright." Oliver started to stand up.

"No, thanks. I'll be fine." As I turned and walked away, I felt the distance between us lengthening. Which each step that carried me away from him, I felt a sharp pinprick in my heart. What had I done? What had I gotten myself into?

When I reached the door of the cafeteria, I looked back over my shoulder.

Oliver turned his head in the same moment and met my eyes. Even across a large space, his gaze managed to see into the depths of me. His eyes lingered for a moment, then he looked away.

He wasn't going to chase me this time. Not after the way that I'd treated him. Not after I'd insisted that there could never be anything between us. I'd threatened to get him into trouble if he continued to pursue me.

I closed my eyes as I recalled that moment. I'd pushed him so far away that there likely wasn't a way to get back.

It was clear in my mind that I wanted to be with him, no matter what that might take. But the question was, could I handle it? Could I really forgo my rules and dive deep into a relationship with him that I'd been fighting since the first moment I'd met him?

Now that I knew what it felt like to truly be in love, the idea of losing that feeling scared me more than dating in high school ever had. I didn't want to spend my life regretting what might have been. I didn't want to wake up one day in the future and realize that this was my only chance at true love.

My stomach twisted as I came to the realization that I had to at least try. I had to give whatever existed between Oliver and me the opportunity to grow and see where it led us. The question was, after the way I'd treated Oliver, would he even still be interested?

I recalled the words he'd spoken to me at lunch. He said he would do anything. But did he mean that? Was it just something to say? Was I reading too much into it?

There was only one way to find out. My heart fluttered with fear as I realized that I would have to put everything on the line and risk rejection. There was no way to step cautiously into this, I would have to jump in with both feet and hope that it wasn't already too late. But how?

I turned back toward the cafeteria and considered the option of simply running back in and throwing myself into his arms. The very thought left me shaken. I couldn't take a risk like that. What if he rejected me in front of everyone?

No, if I was going to try to connect with Oliver, I had to be smart about it. I had to have a plan.

THIRTY-THREE

A few hours later, I held my phone in my hand and stared at the keyboard on the screen. I'd already typed three messages only to delete them. If I wanted to test the waters, I had to say just the right thing. I didn't want to leave myself exposed.

Finally, I began to type a fourth message.

YOU MENTIONED that you might be able to help Jenny. Do you want to meet up and tell me more about it?

I READ THE WORDS OVER. Was there any hint of why I really wanted to see him?

Satisfied that it was vague enough, I sent the message. Then I began to pace around my bedroom.

Would he answer? I wouldn't blame him if he didn't. I hadn't given him any good reason to. But he'd claimed that he wanted to be friends and he'd offered to help, so I held out hope that he would.

But how long would it take? I glanced at the clock on my

bedside table. Two minutes had gone by since I'd sent the message. Had he even read it?

I picked up my phone to make sure that the message had gone through. As I did, my phone buzzed. I looked down to read the message.

COURTYARD IN FIVE MINUTES?

MY HEART JUMPED into my throat. I hadn't expected him to answer so fast or to want to meet up so fast. A few excuses to get out of meeting him popped up in my mind.

None would work. I'd just asked him to meet me; I couldn't beg out of it now.

With shaky finger, I typed out a response.

SEE YOU THERE.

YES, that was casual enough, wasn't it?

I glanced in the mirror and took a minute to run my fingers through my hair. Then I thought better of it and shook it out so it would be messy again. I didn't want to give him the impression that I'd taken the time to fix my hair before I met him. I didn't want to give him any indication that I might actually be interested, even though just the thought of seeing him left me beside myself with eagerness.

I let five minutes slip by, then waited for another two. As I walked down the hall toward the courtyard, I wondered if he would still be there. Would he have given up and left? Would he be annoyed that I was late?

My mind spun with so many different thoughts that I couldn't decide whether I was happy, terrified, or excited. All I knew for sure was that I had to keep going.

I spotted him sitting on a bench in the middle of the courtyard. The sight of him took my breath away. Yes, there he was, within reach. I could walk up to him and tell him exactly how I felt.

The words bubbled up in my throat, ready to be spoken. But before I could voice them, I clenched my teeth shut tight. I wouldn't allow myself to get out of control. I had to be in charge of my emotions and take each step as cautiously as possible.

"There you are." He smiled as he looked at me. "I thought you might have gotten distracted."

"Nothing could distract me." I sat down beside him.

"Of course not, not with Jenny's future on the line."

"Right." I chewed on my bottom lip, then focused on my hands folded in my lap. "So, what do you think you can do for her?"

"I have my father leaning on the admissions administrator. I'm sure that he'll be able to convince them to let her back in."

"Why is he willing to help?" I met his eyes.

"I told him it was important to me. He takes that seriously."

"He sounds like a wonderful father to support you that much."

"He is." He cleared his throat. "When he insisted I come to America to get me away from Shauna for a little while, I thought he was cruel. But now I see why he did it."

"Why?" I looked over at him.

"Because he knew that all I needed was some distance—a chance to open my eyes a little wider to see that Shauna wasn't the person that I thought she was." He frowned.

"Do you really believe that?" I shifted closer to him on the bench. "Can you really let go of everything you shared so easily?"

"She's the one that let go, not me." He looked back at me, his eyes narrowed. "I gave her my trust and she cheated on me. She made that choice."

"But you were willing to take her back." My heart skipped a beat as I wondered if he saw me the same way he saw Shauna. I made the choice to let him go. Would it be too late now for me to change my mind?

"I was willing to take her back because I thought I was in love, Maby." He smiled some as he looked out over the court-yard. "I remember you telling me that I couldn't know what real love was, that I was too young. That made me so angry." His hands curved into fists. "It hurt because I was so sure that I was in love with Shauna. But then you went ahead and proved me wrong."

"What do you mean?" I studied him as he turned his attention back to me.

"I mean, you proved to me that I didn't know what true love was. You opened my eyes wider. You showed me that I can feel something much deeper than I ever imagined." He frowned as he shifted away from me on the bench. "I know you don't want to hear me say that."

I felt the words rush up to the tip of my tongue. I could admit the truth. I could admit that I knew exactly what he meant because I felt the same way. But before I could speak them, fear took over. What if I told him and he still decided to go back to England? Could I survive that?

As he continued to speak, I couldn't even hear the words he said. My focus remained on the possibility that I could tell him the truth.

"Ollie." I placed my hand over his as I looked into his eyes.

"Yes?" He smiled. "I like being Ollie again. I guess I've earned my way back into your good graces?"

"I want to thank you for helping me. Jenny is like a sister to me and having her back by my side will make everything better."

"Like I said, anything for you." He wrapped his fingers around my hand and gave it a light squeeze. "That doesn't frighten you, does it?"

"No." I whispered the word as his grip tightened on my hand.

"Maby, I have no interest in making things hard on you. You've made it clear what you don't want to happen between us. I'd hoped that you were right, and that the less we saw each other, the less strongly I would feel about you. But that hasn't happened." He paused as he traced his fingertips along the back of my hand. "I don't think it ever will."

"Ollie." I sighed as I drew my hand back.

"It's alright. It's not your fault. It's mine." He stood up from the bench. "I'm leaving on Monday. I'll make sure things are handled for Jenny before then."

"You're leaving?" I stood up as well and reached for his hand.

"I can't endure this again." He drew back from my touch. "I can't keep the distance you want me to, and I know that's not fair to you. So, I've made arrangements to go back home."

"Ollie, you don't have to do that." My heart raced at the thought of saying goodbye to him.

"It's for the best. For both of us." He frowned as he studied me. "I just can't let you go and I don't want to be a reason for stress in your life. I don't want to be someone that's holding you back from what you really want." He shook his head. "If I've learned anything from all this, it's that no matter how I feel, I can't make anyone else feel the same way." He licked his lips, then met my eyes. "In fact, I think it's probably best if we let this be the last time we talk. Otherwise, it may be too hard for me to go."

"Ollie, it doesn't have to be like this." I tried to catch his hand again, but he took a step back before I could.

"It does. I'm afraid it does." He sighed. "I wish it didn't have to be. I wish I was strong enough to ignore these feelings and be the friend that you deserve, but I'm just not. I'm sorry." He turned and walked off across the courtyard.

THIRTY-FOUR

It felt as if my feet were bolted into the cobblestones beneath me. My body yearned to go after him, but my feet refused to cooperate. I opened my mouth to call out, but all that came out was a strangled squeak.

What could I say? *Oops? I was wrong?*

As my mind spun with panic, a part of me realized that Oliver was right. He was right to walk away. It was what I'd wanted from the first moment I'd realized that I had feelings for him. I wanted to be free of all of it and would have done anything to avoid facing the truth. I wanted to be angry with him for walking away, but the truth was, he was doing it as a kindness. Even in his heartbreak, he thought of me first.

My stomach twisted with the knowledge that if he had just tried to kiss me, I would have given in and kissed him. I would have told him the truth. But he hadn't, probably out of respect for me. Somehow that made everything so much worse.

I sank back down on the bench and closed my eyes as tears brewed within them. Yes, I was in high school. Yes, I still had a lot to learn about life and relationships. But none of that could convince me that the searing pain that ached through me wasn't real. It was the most real thing I'd ever experienced and I felt as if it might overtake me.

I gripped the edge of the stone bench as tight as I could. As the rough surface dug into my skin, I thought about all the times that I'd felt out of control in my life, all of the ways that I'd hidden from any real emotions.

I'd listened to my mother's advice and avoided the pitfalls of romance. I'd also watched all my friends pair up and experience a kind of bliss that I couldn't even imagine. While I'd advised them through their difficult times, I always felt lucky not to be wrapped up in the drama that they were experiencing.

But now, I wished I could be more like them. I wished that I'd never fought the feelings that I had for Oliver. If only I'd been more open to the idea, I might have been able to experience something phenomenal. Instead, I only knew how terrible it felt to think about saying goodbye to him.

It dawned on me just then that I hadn't even said goodbye. He'd walked away and I hadn't even been able to say those words to him. He deserved so much more.

"No, I can't let this happen." I stood up from the bench and looked in the direction that he'd walked. It didn't matter if his tickets had already been purchased, if he'd already made whatever arrangements were needed, I had to get to him before he left the country. Not just get to him but get through to him. I had to prove to him that I felt the same way about him and that our relationship was worth staying for.

I couldn't just walk up to him empty-handed. I had to do something to really get his attention, to really convince him that I meant what I said. But in order to do that, I would need some help.

As I hurried back to my dorm room, I knew that I needed my friends more than I ever had. I just hoped that they would be willing to help.

When I burst into my dorm room, I found Fifi there, her nose buried in one of her favorite books.

She dropped it the moment she saw me.

"Maby? What's wrong?" The urgency in her voice made it clear that I must have looked wild.

I felt wild. I felt panicked as I thought about the possibility that Oliver might leave the country before I ever had the chance to tell him the truth, before I had the chance to find out if there could be something real between us.

"Fi!" I gasped out her name as I sank down on the sofa. "I've made a terrible mistake."

"Maby, just breathe." She wrapped her arms around me. "Whatever it is, it can't be that bad. We'll figure it out together, okay?" She tried to meet my eyes. "It's going to be just fine."

"No, I don't think it will be." I winced as tears began to slide down my cheeks. "I think it's too late. I've messed everything up."

"I don't believe that for a second." She cupped my cheeks and looked into my eyes. "Take a deep breath, we're going to figure it out."

As I finally met her eyes and took the deep breaths she told me to, all my fears rushed to the surface.

"I just didn't want to get hurt, Fi. I just wanted to protect myself. I didn't realize how foolish I was being."

"This is about Oliver, isn't it?" Her eyes widened. "Oh, Maby, you poor thing." She hugged me tighter.

"He's going back to England, Fi. I'll never see him again."

"Sh. Don't worry about that now." She stroked my hair. "He's not going to go anywhere without you."

"What do you mean?" I pulled back far enough to look at her.

"I mean, you're not alone in the way you're feeling. I can see by the way he looks at you that he feels the same way about you. All you have to do is tell him."

"No, I don't think that will be enough." I pulled away from her and began to pace back and forth throughout the room. "I need to do something to get his attention, to prove that I really do feel the way I say I do. Otherwise he'll never believe me."

"I just don't think that's true. You don't need to prove yourself to him." Fifi caught my hand and stopped me from pacing. "All you have to do is tell him the truth and he's going to be thrilled."

"You weren't there." I frowned as I looked at her. "You didn't see him walk away. I did. I've had so many chances to tell him the truth and instead, I've lied through my teeth. He's not going to believe me. He's going to tell me it's too late and go back to England and then I'll be left here, heartbroken and alone."

"You won't be alone." Fifi hugged me. "Not ever. If you want to do something to prove yourself, then I'll help you. But I really don't think you have to."

"I've been trying to come up with something that will be just right." I sighed as I sat back down on the sofa. "Something special that will remind him of our connection."

"Maybe a special moment you shared?" Fifi sat down next to me. "Was there a time when you realized how you really felt?"

"At the stables!" I jumped back up. "That's it! It needs to be at the stables. He rescued me and we stood in the rain together." I glanced out the window. "It's sunny out, but it will have to do. Now I just need to think of a way to get him there."

"Maybe Aaron would help us?" Fifi pursed her lips. "I'll bet he would, if we asked."

"Yes! Aaron!" I pulled out my phone and dialed the number for the stables. As I waited for him to answer, my plan began to come together.

"Hello?"

"Aaron, it's Mabel. Do you think you could help me out with something?"

"Sure. What do you need?"

I took a deep breath, then launched into my idea. Once he agreed, I hung up the phone. I typed out a text to Oliver. Instead of rewriting it over and over again, I sent it right away.

OLIVER, I didn't say goodbye. Could you please meet me at the stables in an hour? I'll be waiting.

THIRTY-FIVE

As I stared at my phone, I hoped that he would respond instantly.

Several minutes slid by with no answer.

"I don't know if he's going to be there." I frowned as I glanced up at Fifi.

"He'll be there." She smiled as she led me toward the door. "Let's make sure you're there and ready when he arrives."

"Do you think this is silly?" I sighed as I followed her out the door. "Maybe I'm just being ridiculous."

"Not at all." She led me down the stairs toward the common room. "I think it's romantic and there's nothing wrong with that, Maby. Trust me, he's going to be so happy to see you."

I thought about that possibility. I imagined him meeting my eyes and knowing that the time had finally come for us to kiss. He would help me down off the horse and into his arms and everything would be just fine—better than fine—wonderful.

As much as I wanted to believe that was what would happen, I worried that it would actually be far different.

Maybe he'd get there and just want me to say goodbye. Maybe he'd help me down from the horse, pull me into his arms, and say that he wished things could have turned out differently."

I winced at that possibility. How would I survive that?

Worse, what if he didn't show up at all? My chest ached at the thought.

I checked my phone again. Still no response. Even with Fifi beside me in the taxi, I still felt very alone. Was this how it would be from now on? Would I always feel this way?

"Ugh, I'm a mess." I looked over at her. "He's not answering. What if he doesn't come?"

"Relax." She patted my knee and smiled. "I'm pretty sure Oliver would do absolutely anything to be there. Soon enough you'll have your answer."

I wished that I could feel as confident as Fifi sounded. But that was her job, wasn't it? She had to tell me that everything was going to be alright. As my friend, she would be as positive as possible. I was not feeling positive. Not even close.

When we arrived at the stable, Aaron met us.

"So far so good?" He smiled at me.

"I'm not sure." I frowned as I shoved my hands into my pockets. "This might not work out after all."

"I made sure the horses are ready." He tipped his head toward the corral. "When he gets here, I'll make sure he gets Clover."

"Don't worry, I'm here!" Candy shouted as she ran down the driveway with a picnic basket in her hands. "Sorry, I had to do a bit of running around to find some real English-style cuisine, but I got it!"

"Candy?" My eyes widened as I looked at her.

"I recruited a bit of help." Fifi smiled. "I thought you two might like to share a picnic."

"You two are amazing." I hugged them both. "Candy, I hope you're not upset with me."

"Not at all. I knew you two had a connection from the start. I'm just glad that you're willing to admit it and see where it goes."

"It might be going nowhere." I frowned as I checked my phone again. "I still haven't heard from him."

"He'll be here." Fifi met my eyes. "Try not to worry." She glanced over at Candy. "We should go—let the lovebirds have their time together."

"Good idea."

I winced at the term. Was that what I was? Some silly creature flitting through the air?

As much as I didn't want to admit it, I knew that it was true. My heart beat as fast as any bird's wings and the very thought of seeing Oliver made my mind swirl with excitement. I did my best to hide this by forcing a frown as I waved to my friends.

With the picnic basket placed in front of me, I rode Goldie down the same path that we'd taken on the day that she'd been frightened by the storm. A glance up at the sky revealed that it was still bright and sunny. No, I wouldn't be able to recreate the exact moment, but at least it would be a beautiful day.

I guided Goldie toward the patch of trees that Oliver and I had stood under that day, then slid down off the horse. As I spread out the blanket on the grass nearby, I tried to resist checking my phone. Maybe he hadn't even gotten my text yet. I doubted that. He'd never left me waiting when I texted him.

Once the picnic basket was on the blanket, I pulled my phone from my pocket. My heart dropped as I saw no new messages from him.

"Maybe Fifi was right, maybe I already have my answer." I frowned as I stared at the screen. I couldn't blame him if he didn't show up. He'd already made up his mind to leave and I was the one who'd asked him to go. So why should he risk seeing me again?

I thought about sending another message, pleading with him to show up, but I decided against it. If he had decided not to come, there was nothing I could say to change his mind.

I sat down on the blanket and took a few calming breaths. There was still time for him to arrive. I just needed to keep an open mind.

I thought about all the time we'd spent together. He constantly challenged me, which I found infuriating at first, but now I craved it. He had seen the truth inside of me, when even I refused to see it. He knew that my rules wouldn't stop me. I felt like he had opened me up and now there was no way to shut everything down again. Whether he showed up or not, he had permanently changed me. Was it for the better?

I stared up at the clouds drifting across the sky and hoped that was true.

As more time slid by, calming breaths did nothing to help my mounting frustration. He hadn't texted me back. He hadn't shown up at the stables.

I began to fold up the picnic blanket. It was clear that his lack of response was an answer. Still, the thought of climbing onto Goldie and riding back to the stable made me feel even worse. Maybe if I waited just a little longer, he would change his mind and show up. I couldn't sit still.

Instead of pacing, I began to walk a nearby trail. It was a narrow path that led to a small stream. I could recall walking it with Jenny a few times. She always called it a romantic place because it was hard to find, and when you went around one bend in the trail, the stream appeared out of nowhere. She called it magical.

"I need some of that magic now, Jenny." I shoved my hands into my pockets and tried to imagine my friend right beside me. She would give me a shove, tell me to stop being so serious, and then run off, forcing me to chase her. She had such a spontaneous nature and a zest for life that a part of me envied.

The thought of her made me smile. No matter what, I had amazing friends and that was something I would always be grateful for.

More time passed. It was clear that he wasn't coming.

I sighed as I rounded the bend and neared the stream. The sun sparkled on its surface; the water rushed past, dedicated to its journey. But Oliver didn't magically appear.

Disappointed, I walked back down the path. As I neared the end of it, I closed my eyes and prepared myself for the reality I would have to face. Oliver had moved on; he'd made his decision and that was something that I would have to find a way to live with. Tears began to flow down my cheeks as the harsh truth of that took root in my heart.

Suddenly, I needed to run. I needed to get as far from the stables as I could, before anyone could see me. With my eyes squeezed shut in an attempt to hold back my tears, I launched myself forward, then slammed into something warm and solid.

A chest?

"Maby?" Someone sputtered out my name as the person stumbled back.

I looked up to see who I'd bumped into. Who would be out in the woods in the exact same place I was?

THIRTY-SIX

It was one more thing that had gone wrong with my day. One more reminder that nothing was going smoothly for me. Annoyed, I was ready to snap at whoever dared to step in my way. I was also mortified. I didn't want anyone to see me. I wanted to hide. The tears that streaked down my cheeks would give away the truth to anyone who was paying attention.

With my heart in my throat, I looked up at the person I'd bumped into, prepared to launch into a lecture about being more careful about looking where they were going.

As I caught sight of his familiar face, my chest tightened and my breath grew short. Was it possible? Or had I just imagined his presence? Nervously, I met his eyes. Was he here because he wanted to be or had he shown up out of kindness?

"Ollie?" I took a sharp breath as I pressed one hand against the curve of his arm to make sure that he was real.

"Hi there. Are you okay?" He trailed his fingertips through the tears on my cheek.

"I thought you weren't coming." My heart raced as I realized that it was real. He was definitely there and he didn't seem to be interested in leaving any time soon. His touch comforted me in the same moment that it frightened me. He had shown up. Now I had to do my part.

"I thought you'd already left. Then I saw Goldie tied up back there and I hoped maybe I'd find you." He stared into my eyes. "I know I'm late, I'm sorry. I didn't think you would wait for me."

"Ollie, I've been waiting for you for a long time." I bit into my bottom lip. "All this time, I've told myself that it was best to wait, wait until I was ready for something real. I'm so glad I did, because it—because you are worth the wait."

"What are you saying?" He brushed my hair back from my eyes and stepped closer to me.

"I'm sorry if it's too late." Tears blurred my vision. "I'm so sorry that I fought this so hard—and if I hurt you." I caressed his cheek as a shiver carried through my body. "I never meant to do that."

"Maby." He frowned as he caught my hand, then pressed it against his chest. "You haven't hurt me. You've set me free."

"Ollie." I winced. I didn't want him to be free, I didn't want him to move on and go back to England. I wanted him to be with me.

"You opened my eyes." He covered my hand with his own and continued to hold it against his chest. "I never knew what real love was until the day I met you, Maby."

"Me either." I gulped down a breath. I could feel his heartbeat pound against my palm. It quickened when I looked into his eyes. "Ollie, I know it's not fair of me to ask, I know that I'm the reason for all the chaos between us, but I don't want you to go."

"Maby." He whispered my name as his head tipped toward mine.

"Ollie, please." My forehead touched his as I whispered as well. "Please stay."

The fingertips of his free hand glided through my hair. He tangled the locks around his hand and tickled his touch along the back of my neck. Every light caress sent a new bolt of electricity through my skin.

My mind swam, awash with the desire that his closeness inspired in me. I had fantasized so many times about what it would be like to kiss him, to feel his arms around me, for him to hold me with no intention of ever letting go, but in that moment, I realized that none of those fantasies could ever come close to the real thing. My body buzzed from head to toe and the air between us became so thick with passion that I felt as if I was breathing in the essence of what we felt for each other.

This wasn't some silly high school crush. It wasn't a dream that I could live in for a few minutes and then abandon for the sake of safety. The feeling of his skin, as he slid his head to the side and brushed his cheek against mine, was full of danger and potential. I knew that this was my chance. If I let fear overtake me, if I let it drive me into pulling away, I would never know the sweetness of his kiss.

While my heart raced with anticipation, my muscles tensed with fear. What if he ducked away and told me it was already too late? What if he we kissed and he realized he didn't really feel the same way?

He leaned back, his cheek abandoning mine. He let his hand fall away from me and settle against his chest. His other hand remained tangled in my hair as he gazed into my eyes.

"Maby." His lips quivered as he spoke my name. "I will always be right here. I'll never walk away. I will always stay."

At those words, I could no longer resist. All desire to run from his touch vanished and my lips headed toward his. I wrapped my arms around his neck and felt a shiver course through him as my mouth neared his.

Then it happened. As if it had been planned to happen just this way for as long as I'd been alive.

I pressed my lips to his and the entire world swirled around me. It was as soft and sweet as I imagined, but so much more. Warmth filled every inch of my body and spilled out in the eagerness of my kiss.

Instead of pulling away, I tightened my arms around him. I felt as if I could kiss him forever.

He must have felt the same way, because the moment my lips broke free of his, he chased them down and drew them back into another heavy kiss.

Overwhelmed by my passion for him I swayed forward into his arms. I leaned against his chest and felt his arms wrap around my waist. In that moment, I felt as if the sun shone just for the two of us.

I had no idea what the future might hold. Would he eventually want to go back to England? Would I want to go with him? Would our lives take separate paths? With his arms around me, I couldn't even imagine that possibility.

One thing I knew for certain, no matter what happened as our lives continued on, I would never regret breaking my rule and falling for a boy in high school. Maybe it still didn't make sense to me, but it didn't have to.

"I was trying to text you back." He brushed his lips across my cheek and whispered. "I was so excited to get your message. I tried to respond, but I dropped my phone and it fell behind my desk. I tried to get it back. I thought if I didn't respond you might think I didn't want to be here. It took me forever and I couldn't get to it. I'm so sorry that I kept you waiting." He met my eyes.

"Don't be so sorry." I brushed my fingers through his hair and smiled. "I waited. I would have waited even longer. You are worth the wait, Ollie."

As I kissed him again, I realized that was true. For all the times I'd avoided dating—for all the times I'd told myself that it was for the best to remain alone while all my friends were falling in love—now I could see that I was right.

I wanted it to be the right moment with the right person and finally that moment had arrived. And Oliver was more than worth the wait. He was everything I'd ever dreamed of.

EPILOGUE

"Keep up!" Oliver shouted back over his shoulder at me as Clover raced forward.

"Let's go, Goldie." I leaned forward toward the horse's mane as I urged her to quicken her gallop.

Oliver threw his head back and laughed as he maintained a short distance ahead of me. "You're never going to catch me, are you?"

My heart raced at the thought. "I'm right behind you! Just wait!"

"We'll see!" He winked at me, then guided Clover into a jump over a low fence.

Goldie jumped into the air and cleared the fence right behind them.

Over the past few months, I'd discovered what it was like to be truly, madly in love. Oliver still challenged me at every turn, but he also guided me through the ups and downs of our relationship.

At first, every little squabble made me think that it would be over. But he showed me that as promised, he would stay, and I learned to be patient and to trust that we could navigate any hurdle that we faced.

As Goldie finally pulled up beside him, he glanced over at me.

"Oh, there you are." He grinned. "I was wondering when you might show up."

"Now, see if you can catch me...!" I flashed him a smile as Goldie pulled past him and continued toward the stables.

Oliver and I spent a lot of our time riding, and lately we hadn't been out on the trails alone.

"Are you two ever going to catch up?" Jenny called out from her horse as she glanced back at us. "Slowpokes!"

"How does she get that horse to go so fast?" Oliver shook his head as he laughed. "She's amazing."

"Yes, she is." I eased Goldie into a trot right beside Clover and reached for Oliver's hand. "And so are you."

"I am, aren't I?" He smiled as he leaned over to kiss the back of my hand. "You are so very lucky."

"I am!" I laughed and swatted at him as I pulled my hand away.

After we caught up with Jenny, I slid down from the saddle and walked Goldie over to a post near the stable.

"You win—again." I rolled my eyes.

"I can't help it." Jenny smiled as she tied her own horse up as well. "I love feeling the breeze in my hair. Being cooped up at my aunt's house was no fun at all. It's great to be back here. I just wish everyone felt the same way."

I noticed a shadow in her expression. That shadow was never there before. My once bright and cheerful friend hadn't exactly been welcomed back to Oak Brook with open arms. She'd faced some resistance from the other students. I wished there was a way I could erase her pain, but I knew it wasn't possible. Still, I hugged her and held her close against me.

"Jenny, I'm going to tell you a secret."

"You are?" She smiled as she looked at me. "But we're not in the right place to tell secrets."

"It's alright, I don't need to whisper it." I watched as Oliver led his horse over to a trough for a drink.

"So? What's the secret?" She raised an eyebrow.

"One day you're going to meet someone, someone absolutely wonderful. When you do, nothing that anyone else thinks is going to matter to you." I tipped my head toward Oliver. "Trust me, I know."

"That's sweet, Maby." She smiled as she looked over at Oliver. "He really is a great guy. But that's just not in the cards for me."

"What do you mean?" I met her eyes. "Don't you want to fall in love?"

"No." She pursed her lips. "I don't think anyone could understand what I've been through over the past year. I don't think I want to explain it. I just want to be on my own for a while."

"I can understand that. But I'm living proof that things don't always work out that way." I smiled as I recalled how hard I'd fought to deny my feelings for Oliver. "I would suggest that you keep your heart open. See where it leads. Don't make the same mistakes I did."

"Hm...well, it all seems to have worked out pretty well for you." She offered that infectious smile and nudged my shoulder with hers. "Everything happens at the right time, right? I'm just pretty sure that this isn't the right time for me. Maybe one day, though. Maybe." She shrugged. "Your romance turned out to be pretty great. Mine didn't. As much as I believe in love, I'm not sure that I'll want to take that risk again for a long time."

"Whatever you need, I'll be here for you." I hugged her.

"I know you will be, Maby." She smiled as she looked into

my eyes. "Now go snuggle up to that adorable little creature before he gets too lonely without you." She gave me a light shove toward Oliver.

I laughed as I walked over to him. Even as his arms wrapped around me, I looked back over my shoulder at Jenny. Now that I knew just how wonderful it could feel to be in love, I hoped that my best friend would be able to experience that for herself one day. Until then, I intended to be the best friend I could to her.

"I love you, Maby." Oliver leaned his forehead against mine.

"I love you too, Ollie." I closed my eyes and savored the moment.

ALSO BY JILLIAN ADAMS

Amazon.com/author/jillianadams

OAK BROOK ACADEMY SERIES

The New Girl (Sophie and Wes)

Falling for Him (Alana and Mick)

No More Hiding (Apple and Ty)

Worth the Wait (Maby and Oliver)

A Fresh Start (Jennifer and Gabriel)

Made in the USA
Middletown, DE
12 May 2020